"I need some help."

"You!" Mandelyn burst out.

Carson glared at her. "Don't make jokes."

"Okay." She sighed. "What do you want me to do?"

He hesitated uncharacteristically. His face hardened. "Hell, look at me," he growled finally, ramming his hands into the pockets of his worn, faded jeans. "You told Patty I was too savage to get a woman, and you were right. I don't know how to behave in civilized company. I don't even know which fork to use in a fancy restaurant." He shifted restlessly, looking arrogant and proud and self-conscious all at once. "I want you to teach me some manners."

"Me?" Mandelyn exclaimed in shock.

"Of course you," he shot back. "There's no one else who could teach me as well as you could."

Also available from MIRA Books and
DIANA PALMER

THE RAWHIDE MAN
LADY LOVE

Coming soon

FRIENDS AND LOVERS

DIANA PALMER

Cattleman's Choice

MIRA BOOKS

ISBN 1-55166-056-3

CATTLEMAN'S CHOICE

Printed in U.S.A.

For Alicia
And for Arizona's Stephanie, Ellen, Trish and Nita

Chapter One

At first, Mandelyn thought the pounding was just in her head; she'd gone to bed with a nagging headache. But when it got louder, she sat up in bed with a frown and stared at the clock. The glowing face told her that it was one o'clock in the morning, and she couldn't imagine that any of the ranch hands would want to wake her at that hour without cause.

She jumped up, running a hand through the glorious blond tangle of her long hair, and pulled on a long white robe over her nightgown. Her soft gray eyes were troubled as she wound through the long ranchstyle house to the front door that overlooked the Chiricahua Mountains of southeastern Arizona.

"Who is it?" she asked in the soft, cultured tones of her Charleston upbringing.

"Jake Wells, ma'am," came the answer.

That was Carson Wayne's foreman. And without a single word of explanation, she knew what was wrong, and why she'd been awakened.

She opened the door and fixed the tall, blond man with a rueful smile. "Where is he?" she asked.

He took off his hat with a sigh. "In town," he replied. "At the Rodeo bar."

"Is he drunk?" she asked warily.

The foreman hesitated. One corner of his mouth went up. "Yes, ma'am," he said finally.

"That's the second time in the last two months," she said with flashing gray eyes.

Jake shrugged, turning his hat around in his hands. "Maybe money's getting tight," he guessed.

"It's been tight before. And it isn't as if he doesn't have options, either," she grumbled, turning. "I've had a buyer for that forty-acre tract of his for months. He won't even discuss it."

"Miss Bush, you know how he feels about those condominium complexes," he reminded her. "That land's been in his family since the Civil War."

"He's got thousands of acres!" she burst out. "He wouldn't miss forty!"

"Well, that particular forty is where the old fort stands."

"Nobody's likely to use it these days," she said with venom.

He only shrugged, and she went off to change her clothes. Minutes later, dressed in a yellow sweater and designer jeans, she drew on her suede jacket and went out to climb in beside Jake in the black pickup truck with the Circle Bar W logo of Carson Wayne's cattle company emblazoned in red on the door.

"Why doesn't anybody else ever get called

to go save people from him?'' she asked curtly.

Jake glanced at her with a faint smile. ''Because you're the only person in the valley who isn't scared of him.''

''You and the boys could bring him home,'' she suggested.

''We tried once. Doctor bills got too expensive.'' He grinned. ''He won't hit you.''

That was true enough. Carson indulged her. He was fiery and rough and lived like a hermit in that faded frame building he called a house. He hated neighbors and he was as savage a man as she'd ever known. But from the first, he'd warmed to her. People said it was because she was from Charleston, South Carolina and a lady and he felt protective of her. That was true, up to a point. But Mandelyn also knew that he liked her because she had the same wild spirit he possessed, because she stood up to him fearlessly. It had been that way from the very beginning.

They wound along the dusty ranch road out to the highway. There was just enough light to see the giant saguaro cacti lifting their arms to the sky, and the dark mountains silhouetted against the horizon. Arizona was beautiful enough to take Mandelyn's breath away, even after eight years as a resident. She'd come from South Carolina at the age of eighteen, devastated by personal tragedy, expecting to find the barren land a perfect expression of her own emotional desolation. But her first sight of the Chiricahua Mountains had changed her mind. Since then, she'd learned to look upon the drastically different vegetation with loving, familiar eyes, and in time the lush green coastline of South Carolina had slowly faded from memory, replaced by the glory of creosote bushes in the rain and the stately stoicism of the saguaro. Her cultured upbringing was still evident in her proud carriage and her soft, delicately accented voice, but she was as much an Arizonian now as a Zane Grey character.

"Why does he do this?" she asked as they wound into the small town of Sweetwater.

"Not my business to guess," came the reply. "But he's a lonely man, and feeling his years."

"He's only thirty-eight," she said. "Hardly a candidate for Medicare."

Jake looked at her speculatively. "He's alone, Miss Bush," he said. "Problems don't get so big when you can share them."

She sighed. How well she knew that. Since her uncle's death four years before, she'd had her share of loneliness. If it hadn't been for her real estate agency, and her involvement in half a dozen organizations, she might have left Sweetwater for good just out of desperation.

Jake parked in front of the Rodeo bar and got out. Mandelyn was on the ground before he could come around the hood. She started toward the door.

The bartender was waiting in the doorway, wringing his apron, his bald head shining in the streetlight.

"Thank God," he said uneasily, glancing behind him. "Mandelyn, he's got a cowboy treed out back."

She stopped, blinking. "He's what?"

"One of the Lazy X's hands said something that set him off. God knows what. He was just sitting quiet at the table, going through a bottle of whiskey, not bothering anybody, and the stupid cowboy..." He stopped on an impatient sigh. "He busted my mirror, again. He broke half a dozen bottles of whiskey. The cowboy had to go to the hospital to get his jaw wired back together...."

"Wait a minute," she said, holding up a hand. "You said he had the cowboy treed..."

"The cowboy whose jaw he broke had friends," the bartender sighed. "Three of them. One is out cold on the floor. Another one is hanging from his jacket on a hook where Carson put him. The third one, the last one, is up in a tree out back of here and Carson is sitting there, grinning, waiting for him to come down again."

Carson never grinned. Not unless he was mad as hell and ready for blood. "Oh, my,"

Mandelyn sighed. "How about the sheriff?"

"Like most sane men, he gave the job of bringing Carson in to his deputy."

Mandelyn lifted her delicate eyebrows. "And?"

"The deputy," the bartender told her, "is in the hall closet, asking very loudly to be let out."

"Why don't you let him out?" she persisted.

"Carson," the bartender replied, "has the key."

"Oh."

Jake pulled his hat low over his eyes. "I'm going to sit in the truck," he said.

"Better go get the bail bondsman out of bed first, Jake," the bartender said darkly.

"Why bother?" Jake asked. "Sheriff Wilson isn't going to get out of bed to arrest the boss, and since Danny's locked in the closet, I'd say it's all over but the crying."

"And the paying," the bartender added.

"He'll pay you. He always does."

The bartender made a harsh sound in his throat. "That doesn't make up for the inconvenience. Having to order mirrors...clean up broken glass...it used to be once every few months, about time his taxes came due. Now it's every month. What's eating him?"

"I wish I knew," Mandelyn sighed. "Well, I'd better go get him."

"Lots of luck," the bartender said curtly. "Watch out. He may have a gun."

"He may need it," she told him with a cold smile.

She walked through the bar, out the back door, just in time to catch the tail end of a long and ardent string of curses. They were delivered by a tall man in a sheepskin coat who was glaring up at a shivering, skinny man in the top of an oak tree.

"Miss Bush," the Lazy X cowboy wailed down at her. "Help!"

The tall, whipcord-lean man turned, pale blue eyes lancing at her from under thick black eyebrows. He was wearing a dark ranch hat pulled low on his forehead, and his lean, tough face needed a shave as much as his thick, ragged hair needed cutting. He had a pistol in one hand and just the look of him would have been enough to frighten most men.

"Go ahead, shoot," she dared him, "and I'll haunt you, you bad-tempered Arizona sidewinder!"

He stood slightly crouched, breathing slowly, watching her.

"If you're not going to use that gun, may I have it?" she asked, nodding toward the weapon.

He didn't move for a long, taut minute. Then he silently flipped the gun, straightening as he held the butt toward her.

She moved forward, taking it gently, carefully. Carson was unpredictable in these moods, but she'd been dealing with him for a long time, now. Long enough to know how to handle him. She emptied the pistol carefully and stuck it in one coat pocket, putting the bullets in the other.

"Why is that man in the tree?" she asked Carson.

"Ask him," Carson said in a deep drawl.

She looked up at the thin cowboy, who was young and battered looking. She recognized him belatedly as one she'd seen often in the grocery store. "Bobby, what did you do?"

The young cowboy sighed. "Well, Miss Bush, I hit him over the back with a chair. He was choking Andy, and I was afraid he was going to do some damage."

"If he apologizes," she said to Carson, who was slightly unsteady on his feet, "can he come down?"

He thought about that for a minute. "I guess."

"Bobby, apologize!" she called up.

"I'm sorry, Mr. Wayne!" came the prompt reply.

Carson glared up toward the limb. "All right, you..."

Mandelyn had to grit her teeth as Carson went through a round of unprintable words before he let the shivering cowboy come down.

"Thanks!" Bobby said quickly, and ran for it, before Carson had time to change his mind.

Mandelyn sighed, staring up at Carson's hard face. It was a long way up. He was tall and broad shouldered, with a physique that would have caught any woman's eye. But he was rough and coarse and only half civilized, and she couldn't imagine any woman being able to live with him.

"Jake with you?" he bit off.

"Yes. As usual." She moved closer and slowly reached out to catch his big hand in hers. It was callused and warm and it made her tingle to touch it. It was an odd reaction, but she didn't stop to question it. "Let's go home, Carson."

He let her lead him around the building, as docile as a lamb, and not for the first time she wondered at that docility. He would have attacked any man who tried to stop him. But for some reason he tolerated Mandelyn's interference. She was the only person his men would call to get him.

"Shame on you," she mumbled.

"Button up," he said curtly. "When I want a sermon, I'll call a preacher."

"Any preacher you called would faint dead away," she shot back. "And don't give me orders, I don't like it."

He stopped suddenly. She was still holding his hand and the action jerked her backward.

"Wildcat," he said huskily, and his eyes glittered in the dim light. "For all your culture and polish, you're as hard as a backcountry woman."

"Sure I am," she replied. "I have to be, to deal with a savage like you!"

Something darkened his eyes, hardened his jaw. All at once, he turned her, whipped her around, and bent to jerk her completely off the ground and into his hard arms.

"Put me down, Carson!" she said curtly, pushing at his broad shoulders.

He ignored her struggles. One of his arms, the one that was under her shoulders, shifted, so that his hand could catch her long blonde hair and pull her head back.

"I'm tired of letting you lead me around like a cowed dog," he said in a gruff undertone. "I'm tired of being called a savage. If that's what you think I am, maybe it's time I lived down to my reputation."

His grip on her hair was painful, and she only half heard the harsh words. Then, with shocking precision, he brought his hard mouth down on her parted lips and took possession.

It was the first time he'd touched her, ever. She went rigid all over at the unfamiliar intimacy of his whiskey-scented mouth, the rasp of whiskers that raked her soft skin. Her eyes, wide open and full of astonished fear, looked up at his drawn eyebrows, at the thick black lashes that lay against his hard, dark-skinned cheek. He made an odd sound, deep in his throat, and increased the pressure of his mouth until it became bruisingly painful.

She protested, a wild sound that penetrated the mists of intoxication and made his head slowly lift.

His chiseled lips were parted, his eyes as shocked as her own, his face harder than ever as he looked down at her. His hard gaze went to her lips. In that ardent fury his teeth had cut the lower one.

All at once, he seemed to sober. He put her gently down onto her shaky legs and hesitantly took her by the shoulders.

"I'm sorry," he said slowly.

She touched her trembling lips, all the fight gone out of her. "You cut my mouth," she whispered.

He reached out an unsteady finger and touched it while his chest lifted unsteadily.

She drew back from that tingling contact, her eyes wide and uncertain.

He let his hand fall. "I don't know why I did that," he said.

She'd never wondered before about his love life, about his women. But the feel of his mouth had fostered an unexpected intimacy between them, and suddenly she was curious about him in ways that unsettled her.

"We'd better go," she said. "Jake will be worried."

She turned, leaving him to follow. She couldn't have borne having to touch him again until some of the rawness subsided.

Jake opened the door, frowning when he saw her face. "You okay?" he asked quickly.

"Just battle-scarred," she replied with a trace of humor. She climbed in, drawing her knees together as a subdued Carson climbed in beside her and slammed the door shut.

"Get going," he told Jake without looking at him.

It was a horrible ride back home for Mandelyn. She felt betrayed. In all their turbulent relationship, she'd never once thought of him in any physical way. He was much too coarse to be an object of desire, too uncivilized and antisocial. She'd vowed that she'd never love a man again, that she'd live on the memory of the love she'd lost so many years ago. And now Carson had shocked her out of her apathy with one brutal kiss. He'd robbed her of her peace of mind. Tonight, he'd changed the rules, without any warning, and she felt empty and raw and a little afraid.

When Jake pulled up at her door, she waited nervously for Carson to get out of the truck.

"Thanks," Jake whispered.

She glanced at him. "Next time, I won't come," she said curtly.

Leaving him to absorb that, she jumped down from the cab and walked stiffly toward the front door without a word to Carson. As she closed the door, she heard the pickup truck roar away. And then she cried.

Chapter Two

When dawn burst over the valley in deep, fiery lights, Mandelyn was still awake. The night before might have been only a dream except for the swollen discomfort of her lower lip, where Carson's teeth had cut it.

She sat idly on the front porch, still dressed, staring vacantly at the mountains. It was spring, and the wildflowers were blooming among the sparse vegetation, but she wasn't even aware of the sparkling early morning beauty.

Her mind had gone back to the first day she'd ever seen Carson, when she was eighteen and had just moved to Sweetwater with her Uncle Dan. She'd gone into the local fast-food restaurant for a soda and Carson had been sitting on a nearby stool.

She remembered her first glimpse of him, how her heart had quickened, because he was the only cowboy she'd seen so far. He was lean and rangy looking, his hair as unruly then as it was now, his face unshaven, his pale eyes insolent and intimate as he lounged back against the counter and stared at her with a blatant lack of good manners.

She'd managed to ignore him at first, but when he'd called to her and asked how she'd like to go out on the town with him, her Scotch-Irish temper had burst through the restraints of her proper upbringing.

Even now, she could remember his astonished look when she'd turned on the stool, coldly ladylike in her neat white suit. She had glared at him from cold gray eyes.

"My name," she'd informed him icily, "is Miss Bush, not, 'hey, honey.' I am not looking for some fun, and if I were, it would not be with a barbarian like you."

His eyebrows had shot up and he'd actually laughed. "Well, well, if it isn't a Southern belle. Where are you from, honey?'

"I'm from Charleston," she said coldly. "That's a city. In South Carolina."

"I made good grades in geography," he replied.

She'd given a mock gasp. "You can read?"

That had set him off. The language that had followed had made her flush wildly, but it hadn't backed her down.

She'd stood up, ignoring the stares of the astonished bystanders, walked straight over to him, and coolly slapped him with all the strength of her slender body behind her small hand. And then she'd walked out the door, leaving him staring at her.

It was days later that she learned they were neighbors. He'd come to talk to Uncle Dan about a horse, and that was when she'd found out who Carson Wayne was. He'd smiled at her, and confessed to her uncle what had happened in town, as if it amused him. It had taken her weeks to get used to Carson's rowdy humor and his unpolished behavior. He would slurp his coffee and ignore his napkin, and use language that embarrassed her. But since he was always around, she had to get used to him. So she did.

Later that first year, she'd gone to the rodeo, and Carson had been beating the stuffing out of another cowboy as she was coming out of the stands. Obviously intoxicated, he was throwing off the men who tried to stop him. Without a thought of defeat, she'd walked over to Carson and touched him lightly on the arm. He'd stopped hitting the other man immediately, looking down at her with dark, quiet eyes. She'd taken his hand, and he'd let her lead him around the corral, to where Jake was waiting nervously. After that, Jake went looking for her whenever his boss went on a spree. And she always went to the rescue. But after last night, she'd never go again.

With a long sigh, she walked back into the house and put on a pot of coffee. She fixed a piece of toast and ate it with her coffee, checking the time. She had a meeting at nine with Patty Hopper, a local woman who'd just come back home fresh out of veterinary school and needed an office. Then, after lunch, she had to talk to the developer who was interested in Carson's forty-acre tract. It was going to be another long day. The man had insisted on seeing Carson personally, but after last night, it was going to be heavy going. Mandelyn didn't particularly relish the thought.

Patty met her at the vacant house Mandelyn wanted to show her. The small, dark-eyed woman had light brown hair and a broad, sweet face. She and Mandelyn had been on the verge of friendship when Patty went away to college, and they still met occasionally when the younger woman was home on vacation.

"Well, what do you think?" Mandelyn answered her. "Isn't it a great location, just off the town square? And I can help you get a great interest rate if you want to finance it over a twenty-year period."

"I'm speechless." Patty grinned warmly. "It's exactly what I wanted. I've got space for an operating room here, and enough acreage out back to put in fences for runs. This gigantic living room will make a perfect waiting room. Yes, I like it. I like the price, too."

"I just happen to have all the paperwork right here," Mandelyn laughed, producing an envelope from her large purse. "Then you can meet with James over at the bank and convince him you need the loan."

"James and I went to school together," Patty told her. "That won't be any problem at all. I've saved up a hefty down payment, and I'm a good credit risk. Just ask all my classmates who loaned me money!"

"I believe you." Mandelyn smiled as she watched Patty sign the preliminary agreement. "This is a sunny office. I can see you making your fortune right here."

"I hope you're right." Patty stood up, folding her arms over the tan sweater she was wearing with casual jeans. "Wow! All mine."

"Yours and the bank's, at least," came the dry reply.

"You're a jewel, Mandy," Patty told her. She glanced curiously at Mandelyn's lip. "I heard you were riding around with Jake in the early morning hours."

"Small towns," Mandelyn said gruffly. "Yes, I was. Carson had the local bar in an uproar again."

Patty laughed. "Just like old times," she said, and looked oddly relieved. "Carson's a bearcat, isn't he? I'm on my way out there next, on a large animal call. He's got a sick bull."

"Don't get too close, he might make a grab for you," Mandelyn teased.

"Me? Not Carson, he's too polite."

"That's rich!" Mandelyn laughed bitterly. "He's a savage. Something right out of ancient history."

"He's always been polite to me," Patty said. "Strange, isn't it, that he's never married?"

Mandelyn felt her blood boil. "It doesn't seem strange to me. He's too uncivilized to get a woman. He'd have to kidnap one and point a gun at her to get a wife!"

"I thought he was your friend," Patty said.

"He was," Mandelyn said coldly. She turned. "Well, I've got a developer coming round in about an hour. I'd better go and have my lunch. I'm glad you liked the office."

"Me too," Patty said, laughing. "Say, do you really think Carson would be all that bad in bed?" she added curiously. "He's awfully sexy."

Mandelyn couldn't meet her friend's eyes. "If you say so. I'll give you a call later about the details of the agreement, okay?" she said with a forced smile.

"Sure," Patty said. "Thanks again."

"My pleasure."

Mandelyn had a salad at the local cafe, but she didn't enjoy it. Her thoughts kept returning to Carson and to Patty's disturbing remarks about him. Afterward, she went back to her office where the developer was pacing back and forth, waiting for her. She made a sly wink at Angie, her new secretary.

"Hello, Mr. Denton," she said pleasantly, extending her hand. "Sorry I'm late. I was finalizing another deal."

"Perfectly all right," he returned, a tall, dignified man in a gray suit. "I'd like to go out to the ranch, if you're ready?"

She hesitated. "I'd better check with Mr. Wayne first," she said.

"I had your secretary do that," he said curtly. "He's waiting for us. I'll drive my car."

She didn't like his high-handedness, but she couldn't afford to antagonize a potential client, so she ground her teeth together in a false smile and followed him out the door.

"Sorry," Angie mouthed at her.

Mandelyn gave her a shrug, and winked again.

All the way to the ranch, Mandelyn felt as if her stomach was tied in knots. She glanced out across the grassy valley rather than ahead to the ramshackle house nestled in the cottonwood trees with the mountains behind it. She didn't want to see Carson. Why was fate tormenting her this way?

His black Thunderbird was sitting near the house, covered with dust and looking unused. The pickup truck Jake had driven the night before was parked by the barn. The corral was deserted. The front door was standing open, but she couldn't see through the screen.

"This is where he lives?" Mr. Denton asked in astonishment as he pulled his green Lincoln up in front of the rough wood house.

"He's rather eccentric," she faltered.

"Crazy," he muttered. He got out of the car, looking neat and alien in his city clothing, and Mandelyn fell reluctantly into step beside him. She was wearing a blue knit suit, with her hair in a bun. She looked elegant and cool, and felt neither. She'd tried to disguise her swollen lip with lipstick, but it was raw where her tongue touched it.

As they started up the steps, Carson walked out onto the porch with quick strides. He looked even taller in his work boots. He was wearing faded denim jeans and a blue chambray shirt half unbuttoned over his broad, hair-roughened chest. He looked tired and hung over, but his blue eyes were alert and at least he seemed approachable.

"Mr. Wayne?" the developer said, putting on his best smile. "Nice place you have here. Rustic."

Carson bent his head to light a cigarette, pointedly ignoring the developer's outstretched hand.

"You won't take no for an answer, will you?" Carson asked him with a cold blue glare.

Denton looked a little ruffled but he withdrew his hand and forced the smile back onto his thin lips. "I got rich that way," he replied. "Look, I'll up my previous offer by two thousand an acre. It's a perfect tract for my retirement village. Lots of water, flat land, beautiful view..."

"It's the best grazing land I've got," Carson replied. "And there's a fort on the place that dates back to the earliest settlement."

"The fort could be moved. I'd be willing..."

"My great-grandfather built it," came the cold reply.

"Mr. Wayne," the developer began.

"Look," Carson said curtly, "I don't like being pushed. This is my place, and I don't want to sell it. I told you that. I told her that," he added, glancing toward Mandelyn. "I'm tired of talking. Come out here again and I'll load my gun."

"You can't threaten me, you backwoods...!" the developer began.

"Oh, no," Mandelyn ground out, covering her face with her hands. She knew even as Carson began cursing what was going to happen. She flinched at the first thud, the shocked cry, the heavy sound of a body landing on hard ground. She peeked between her fingers. The developer was trying to sit up, holding his jaw. Carson was standing over him with calm contempt, smoking his cigarette. He didn't even look rumpled.

"Get off my land, you..." He tacked on a few rough words and bent to lift the other man by the collar. He frog-marched him to the Lincoln, tossed him inside, and slammed the door. "Vamoose!" he growled.

Mandelyn stood there, frozen, while the Lincoln jerked out of the yard. She stared for a long minute and then, with a sigh, started after it.

"Where the hell do you think you're going?" Carson asked.

"Back to town."

"Not yet. I want to talk to you."

She whirled and glared at him. "I don't want to talk to you."

He took her arm and half led, half dragged her up the steps and into the house. "Did I ask?"

"No, you never do!" she shot back. "You just move in and take over! He made you a very generous offer. You've cost me a fortune...!"

"I told you not to bring him out here."

"You told my secretary he could come!" she floundered.

"Like hell I did. I told her to tell him he could come if he felt lucky."

And poor little Angie hadn't realized what that meant.

"Angie's new," she muttered, standing still in the dim living room. He didn't even have electricity. He had kerosene lanterns and furniture that she didn't want to sit on. It looked as if it were made with leftover gunnysacks.

"Sit," he said curtly, dropping into a ragged armchair.

She shifted uncomfortably on her feet. She'd only been in this house once or twice, with her uncle. Since his death, she'd found excuses to stay on the porch or in the yard when she stopped by to talk business with Carson.

His face hardened when he saw the look she was giving the sparse furniture. He got up, furiously angry, and walked into the kitchen.

"In here," he said icily. "Maybe the kitchen chairs will suit you better."

She felt cruel. She hadn't meant to be rude. With a sigh, she walked past him and sat down in one of the cane-bottomed chairs around the table with its red checked oil-cloth cover. "I'm sorry," she said. "I wasn't trying to be rude."

"You didn't want to soil your designer clothes on my filthy furniture," he laughed through narrowed eyes. He sat down roughly and leaned back in the chair, glaring at her. "Why pussyfoot around?"

She stared at him unblinkingly. "What do you want?"

"There's a question," he replied softly. His blue eyes wandered slowly over her face, down to her lips, and hardened visibly. "Hell," he breathed at the swollen evidence of his brutality. He pulled an ashtray toward him with a sigh and crushed out his half-finished cigarette. "I didn't realize how rough I'd been."

"I'll put it down to experience," she said curtly.

"Do you have much?" he asked, holding

her gaze. "Did you fight because you were afraid?"

"You were hurting me!" she said, red with embarrassment and bad temper.

His nostrils flared as he breathed. He paused a moment, and his next words took her completely by surprise. "You told Patty I was too savage to get a woman."

Her mouth flew open. She just sat and stared, hardly able to believe Patty's betrayal.

"I...I never dreamed..."

"That she'd tell me?" he asked coolly. He pulled another cigarette from his pocket and lit it with an impatient snap of his lighter. "She was kidding around, she didn't mean anything. I guess you didn't either." He stared at the cigarette. "I've been thinking about it a lot lately, about getting older, being alone." He looked up. "When Patty said that this morning, it made me mad as hell. Then I realized that you were right, that I don't even know how to behave in polite society. That I'm not...civilized."

"Carson..." she began, at a loss for words.

He shook his head. "Don't apologize. Not for telling the truth." He sighed, stretching, and the hard, heavy muscles of his chest were evident beneath his shirt. Her eyes were drawn to the mat of dark hair visible in the opening, and she felt a sensation that shocked her. "I didn't sleep," he said after a minute, watching her. "I'm sorry I cut your lip, that I manhandled you. I guess you knew I was drinking."

"You tasted of whiskey," she said without thinking, and then flushed when she remembered exactly how he'd tasted.

"Did I?" His eyes dropped to her swollen lip. "I don't know what came over me. And you fought me...that only made it worse. You should have known better, little debutante."

"I've been fighting you for years," she reminded him.

"Verbally," he agreed. "Not physically."

She glared at him. "What was I supposed to do, lie back and enjoy it?" she challenged.

His eyes darkened. His chest rose and fell roughly. "All right, I'm sorry," he growled. "For God's sake, what do you expect? I never knew my mother, never had a sister. My whole life revolved around a man who beat the hell out of me when I disobeyed...."

She stood quietly, forcing away her bad temper, hearing him without thinking until the words began to penetrate. She turned slowly and stared up at him. "Beat you?"

He drew in a slow breath, then glanced down at her bare arm where his strong, tanned fingers held it firmly. His thumb moved on the soft skin experimentally. "My father was a cattleman," he said. "My mother couldn't live with him. She ran away when I was four. He took me in hand, and his idea of discipline was to hit me when I did something he didn't like. I had a struggle just to get through school—he didn't believe in education. But by then, I outweighed him by fifty pounds," he added with glittering eyes, "and I could fight back."

It explained a lot of things. He never talked about his childhood, although she'd heard Jake make veiled references to how rough it had been.

Her eyes searched his hard face curiously.

He lifted his hand to her face and touched her lip gently. "I'm sorry I kissed you like that."

She went flaming red. She felt as if his eyes could see right through her.

"I've never been gentle," he said, "because I never knew what it was to be treated gently. And now, I'm thirty-eight years old, and I'm lonely. And I don't know how to court a woman. Because I'm a savage. This," he sighed bitterly, tracing her swollen lip, "is proof of it."

She stared up at him, searching his eyes quietly as his hand dropped. "Didn't you have any other relatives?" she asked.

"Not one," he said. He turned away and went to stand by the window. "I ran away from home once or twice. He always came after me. Eventually I learned to fight back, and the beatings stopped. But I was four-teen by then. The damage had already been done."

She studied his long back in silence, and then shifted, looking around the messy kitchen until her eyes found a facsimile of a coffee pot. She got to her feet. "Mind if I make some coffee?" she asked. "I'm sort of thirsty."

"Help yourself." He watched her with a familiar, unblinking scrutiny. "You look odd, doing that," he remarked.

"Why?" she asked with a laugh. "I'm very domestic. I cook, too, or don't you re-member those dinners Uncle used to invite you to?"

"It's been years since I've eaten at your table."

She stared down at the pot she was filling. How could she possibly confess that she was too uneasy with him to enjoy his company? He disturbed her, unsettled her and she didn't understand why. Which only made it worse.

"I've been too busy for guests," she said. Her eyes went up to the tattered curtains at the window. "You could use some new curtains."

"I could use a lot of things," he said curtly. "This house is falling apart."

"You're letting it," she reminded him. She put the pot on to boil, grimacing at the grease that had congealed and blackened on top of the once-white range.

"There hasn't been any reason to fix it up before," he said. "Just me, living alone, not much company. But I've hired a construction firm to do some renovations."

That was startling. She turned to face him, her gray eyes wide and curious. "Why?" she asked without thinking.

"It has something to do with the reason I brought you in here," he admitted. He finished the cigarette and crushed it out. "I need some help."

"You!" she burst out.

He glared at her. "Don't make jokes."

"Okay," she sighed. "What do you want me to do?"

He hesitated uncharacteristically. His face hardened. "Hell, look at me," he growled finally, ramming his hands into the pockets of his worn, faded jeans. "You told Patty I was too savage to get a woman, and you were right. I don't know how to behave in civilized company. I don't even know which fork to use in a fancy restaurant." He shifted restlessly, looking arrogant and proud and self-conscious all at once. "I want you to teach me some manners."

"Me?" Mandelyn exclaimed in shock.

"Of course you," he shot back. "Who else do I know with a cultured background? I need educating."

She blinked away her confusion. "After all these years, why now?"

"Females," he said angrily. "You always have to know it all, don't you? Every single damned thing...all right," he sighed roughly, running a hand through his thick hair. "There's a woman."

She didn't know whether to laugh or cry. She stood there like an elegant statue, staring at him. Patty! she thought. It had to be Patty! It was the only possibility that made sense. His unreasonable anger about what Mandelyn had said to Patty, his sudden decision to renovate the house coinciding with Patty's return to Sweetwater. So that was it. The invulnerable man was in love, and he thought Patty had become too citified to like him the way he was. So he was making the supreme sacrifice and having himself turned into a gentleman. Pygmalion in reverse.

"Well?" he persisted, glaring at her. "Yes or no?"

She lifted her shoulders. "Surely there's someone else."

"Not someone like you," he returned. His eyes wandered over her, full of appreciation and something much darker that she missed. "You're quality. A real, honest-to-God lady. No, there's no one else who could teach me as well as you could."

She dropped her eyes to the coffee pot and watched it bubble away.

"Look on it as a challenge," he coaxed. "Something to fill your spare hours. Don't you ever get lonely?"

Her face lifted and she studied him. "Yes," she said. "Especially since Uncle died."

"You don't date?" he said.

She shifted uncomfortably. There was a reason for that, but she didn't want to discuss it with him, not now. "I like my own company."

"It isn't good for a woman to live alone. Haven't you ever thought about getting married?"

"I've thought about a lot of things. What do you want in your coffee?"

She poured it out and braved the refrigerator for cream. Inside there was a basket of eggs, some unsliced bacon, some moldy lumps and what appeared to have been butter at one time.

"I don't have any milk, if that's what you're looking for," he muttered.

She gaped at him. "You have hundreds of cows on this ranch, and you don't have any milk?"

"It isn't a dairy farm," he said.

"A cow is a cow!"

"If you want the damned milk, go milk one of them, then!"

She put her hands on her hips and glared at him. He scowled back. Eventually, she gave in with a sigh and put the cups on the table.

"That's what I like most about you," he said as she sat down gingerly in one of the rickety old chairs.

Her eyes came up. "What?"

He smiled slowly, and his blue eyes darkened, glittered. "You fight me."

Her skin tingled at the way he said it. Before she thought, she said, "You didn't like it last night."

His smile faded. He sighed and lifted the cracked mug to his lips. "I was drunk last night."

"Why?"

He shrugged. "Things got on top of me. I started thinking about how alone I was...." His eyes shot up, pinning hers. "I didn't expect to see you today. I thought you'd never speak to me again."

She fidgeted uncomfortably. "We all get depressed sometimes, even me. It's all right, no harm done." She touched her lower lip with her tongue. "Well, no permanent harm, anyway," she added dryly.

"What you told Patty was true," he said.

"I didn't really mean that, or what I called you last night," she said, watching him. "You're not an unattractive man, Carson."

"Pull the other one," he said curtly and put his cup down to light another cigarette. "I've finally got a little money, and I'm working on some investments that will pay a good dividend. But there's nothing about me that would attract a woman, physically or intellectually, and you know it."

She caught her breath. Did he really believe that? Her eyes wandered slowly over the lean, tough length of him, the powerful muscles of his arms and chest, the narrow flat stomach and long legs. He was devastating physically. Even his craggy face was appealing, if it were shaved and his hair trimmed. She remembered suddenly what Patty had said about how he'd be in bed, and she turned crimson.

He looked up in time to catch that blush and he frowned. "What brought that on?"

She wondered what he'd say if she admitted that she and Patty had been wondering how he was in bed. "Nothing," she said, "just a stray thought."

"Twenty-six, and you still blush like a virgin," he murmured, watching her. "Are you one?" he asked, smiling faintly.

"Carson Joseph Wayne!" she exclaimed.

His blue eyes searched her gray ones. "I didn't realize you knew my middle name."

She toyed with her coffee cup. "It was on the deed, when I sold you that ten-acre parcel that used to be part of Uncle's land."

"Was it?" He sipped some more of his coffee. "You still haven't answered me. Will you teach me?"

She went hot all over at the way he said it. "Carson, any woman who wanted you wouldn't mind the way you are..." she began diplomatically.

"This one would," he said harshly.

She was suddenly jealous and didn't know why. How ridiculous! She touched her temple with a long finger. "Well..."

"I'm not stupid," he said shortly. "I can learn."

"Oh, all right," she said with equal curtness.

He seemed to relax a little. "Great. Where do we start?"

Her eyes wandered over him. God help her, it would take a miracle. "You'll need some new clothes," she said. "A haircut, a shave..."

"What kind of clothes?"

"Shirts and slacks and jeans, and a suit or two."

"What kind? What color?"

She grimaced. "Well, I don't know!"

"You'll have to come with me to Phoenix," he said. "There are some big department stores there."

"Why not Carter's Men's Shop in Sweetwater?" she protested.

His jaw tightened. "No way am I going in there with you, while old man Carter laughs in his whiskers watching us."

She almost laughed at the fierce way he said it. "Okay. Phoenix it is."

"Tomorrow," he added firmly. "It's Saturday," he reminded her when she started to protest. "You can't have any business that won't wait until Monday."

"That sounds as if I'd better not," she laughed.

"You work too hard as it is," he said. "Tomorrow you'll have a holiday. I'll even buy you lunch. You can teach me some table manners at the same time."

It looked like this was going to be a full-time job, but suddenly she didn't mind. The project might be fun at that. After all, Carson did have distinct possibilities. His physique was superb. Why hadn't she ever noticed that? She lifted her cup and sipped her coffee while Carson slurped his.

"That's the first thing," she said, indicating the cup. "Sip, don't slurp."

And when he tried it, unoffended, and succeeded, she grinned at him. He grinned back and a wild flare of sensation tingled up her spine. She'd have to be careful, she told herself. After all, she was revamping him for another woman, not herself. And then she wondered why that was such a depressing thought.

Chapter Three

If it had sounded like a simple thing, helping Carson buy clothes, Mandelyn soon lost her illusions.

"You can't be serious," he told her, glaring as she tried to convince him that a pale blue pinstriped shirt with a white collar was very trendy and chic. "The boys would laugh me out of the yard."

She sighed. "Carson, it's a whole new world. Nobody has to go around in white shirts anymore unless they want to."

"What kind of tie would I wear with that...thing," he asked shortly, while the small salesman hovered nearby chewing on his lower lip.

"A solid one, or something with a small print."

"God save us," Carson burst out.

"And with a solid colored shirt—say, pink—you'd wear a striped tie."

"I'm not wearing pink shirts," he retorted. "I'm a man!"

"A caveman," she agreed. "If you don't want my advice, I'll go buy a tube of lipstick."

"Hold it," he called as she started to walk away. He stared down at the packaged shirt. "All right, I'll get it."

She didn't smile, but it took an effort. Her eyes went over him. He was wearing a beige corduroy jacket and a worn white turtleneck shirt and tan polyester slacks. He'd had a haircut and a shave, though, and already he looked different. In the right clothes, he'd be an absolute knockout, she realized.

After a few minutes, she convinced him that striped shirts weren't at all effeminate, and he bought several more in different colors and ties to match. Then she coaxed him toward the suits.

The salesman took him to the changing rooms, and when he came back minutes later in a vested blue pinstriped suit wearing a blue shirt and burgundy tie, she almost fell off her chair. He didn't look like Carson anymore, except for the rigid features and glittering blue eyes.

"Oh, my," she said softly, staring at him.

His expression softened just a little. "Will I do?" he asked.

"Yes, you'll do," she agreed, smiling. "Women, look out!"

He smiled reluctantly. "Okay, what else do I need?"

"How about something tan?" she asked. "One of those Western-cut suits."

He tried one on, with similar results. He had just the physique to look good in a suit, and the Western cut showed it off to perfection. She let the salesman point him toward some sports coats and slacks, and then after he had paid for his purchases, she talked him into two pairs of new boots and a gray Stetson and a brown one to top it all off.

Just before they left the store she remembered some items they hadn't shopped for. She turned, but she lost her tongue immediately when she tried to say what was on her mind.

His eyebrows arched. "Something wrong?"

"Something we forgot," she said hesitantly.

A corner of his mouth pulled up. "I don't wear pajamas."

"How about things to go under them?" she said finally, averting her eyes.

"My God, you're shy," he laughed, astonished.

"So what?" she returned, her whole stance belligerent. "I've never gone shopping with a man before. And do you have socks?"

"I guess I'd better go back, hadn't I?" He put the parcels in the car. Then he opened the passenger door and helped Mandelyn inside.

"Will you be all right here until I get back?" he asked.

"Sure," she said.

"Won't be a minute."

She watched him walk away, and smiled. Transforming him was getting to be fun, even if it did have its difficult moments.

Her eyes went over the interior of the car. It was spotless, and she guessed that he'd had the boys give it a cleaning for him, because it had never looked so clean. Her hand reached out to touch the silver arrowhead he had suspended from the rear-view mirror and she frowned slightly as she realized what it was attached to. It was a blue velvet ribbon, one she remembered having lost. She'd worn it around her hair in a ponytail one day years ago when Carson had come to see Uncle Dan. She remembered Carson tugging the ponytail, but she hadn't looked back, and later she'd missed the ribbon. It was odd, that a man as unsentimental as Carson would keep such a thing. Perhaps he liked the color, she thought, and turned her eyes back toward the store. It was hot, and there was no shade nearby. She fanned herself with her hand.

Minutes later, he came back, tossed his parcels into the trunk and climbed in beside her.

"I'm sorry, honey," he said suddenly, studying her flushed, perspiring skin. "I didn't expect to be so long. There was a crowd."

She smiled. "I'm okay."

He studied her eyes for a long moment, and his face seemed to go rigid. "Oh, God, you're something," he said under his breath.

The passion in his soft words stirred something deep inside her. She stared back at him and couldn't drag her eyes away. It was a moment out of time. Her eyes dropped involuntarily to his hard mouth.

"Don't," he laughed roughly, turning back to twist the ignition key savagely. "Keep those curious glances to yourself, unless you want me to kiss you again."

He'd shocked her, and her face showed it. She wondered if he wanted her. Then she remembered Patty and went cold. Her eyes gazed out the window. If he had any emotion in him at all, it would naturally be for Patty. Wasn't the object of this whole crusade to make him into a man Patty would want? She crossed her long legs with a sigh and stared out over the city.

"Hungry?" he asked after a minute.

"I could eat a salad," she agreed.

"Rabbit food," he shot back. "You can get that any day."

Her eyebrows arched. "That sounds like you're taking me someplace special," she said, glancing at him with a grin. "Are you?"

"Do you like crepes?" he asked.

Her eyes lit up. "Oh, yes!"

He smiled faintly. "A cattleman I know told me about a place. We'll give it a try."

It turned out to be a hotel restaurant, a very classy one. Mandelyn had definite misgivings about how this was going to turn out, but she'd never be able to teach Carson any manners without going into places like this. So she crossed her fingers and followed him in.

"Do you have a reservation, monsieur?" the maître d' asked with casual politeness, his shrewd eyes going over Carson's worn jacket and polyester trousers. "We are very crowded today."

There were empty tables, Mandelyn could see them, and she knew what was going on. She touched Carson's arm and whispered, "Give him a tip."

"A tip?" Carson growled, glaring down at the shorter man with eyes that threatened to fry him to a crisp. "A tip, hell! I want a table. And I'd better get one fast, sonny, or you and your phony French accent are going right out that front door together." He grinned as he said it, and Mandelyn hid her face in her hands.

"A table for two, monsieur?" the maître d' said with a shaky smile and a quick wave of his hand. "*Mais oui!* Just follow me, *s'il vous plaît!*"

"Tip him, hell," Carson scoffed. "You just have to know the right words to say."

She didn't answer. All around the exclusive dining room, people were staring at them. She tried to follow some distance behind him; maybe she could look as if she were alone.

"Don't hang back there, for God's sake, I'll lose you," Carson said, gripping her arm to half drag her to the table the maître d' was indicating. "Here. Sit down."

He plopped her into a chair and jerked out one for himself, "How about a menu?"

The maître d' turned pink. "Of course. At once."

He signaled a waiter with almost comical haste. "Henri will take care of you, monsieur, mademoiselle," he said, and bowing, beat a hasty retreat.

Henri moved to the table and presented the menus with a flourish. "Would monsieur and mademoiselle like a moment to peruse the menus?" he asked politely.

"Hell, no, we want these crepes," Carson said, pointing at the entry on the menu. "I'll have about five. Get her two, she needs fattening up. And bring us some coffee."

Mandelyn looked under the table, wondering if she might fit beneath it if she tried hard enough.

Henri swallowed. "*Oui,* monsieur. Would you care for a wine list?"

"Hell, what would I do with that?" Carson asked, glaring belligerently at the waiter. "I don't give a damn what kind of wine you've got. Want me to give you a list of my herefords, lot numbers and all? I've got several hundred...."

"I will bring the coffee, monsieur!" the waiter said quickly, and exited.

"This is easy," Carson said, smiling at Mandelyn. "And they say it's hard to get service in fancy restaurants."

She covered her face with her hands again, trying to get her mind settled so that she could explain it to him. But meanwhile, he'd spotted a fellow cattleman across the room.

"Hi, Ben!" he yelled in that deep, slow drawl that carried so well out on the range—and even in this crowded restaurant. "How's that new bull working out? Think your cows will throw some good crossbreeds next spring?"

"Sure hope so, Carson!" the cattleman called back, lifting his wineglass in a salute.

Carson didn't have anything to salute back with, so he raised a hand. "So that's what the wine's for," he told Mandelyn. "To make toasts with. Maybe I better order us a bottle."

"No!" she squeaked, grabbing his hand as he started looking around for Henri.

He stared pointedly at her long, slender hand, which was wrapped around half of his enormous, callused one. "Want to hold hands, do you?" he murmured drily. His fingers caught hers, and all at once the rowdy humor went out of him. He searched her gray eyes. His fingers smoothed over her skin, feeling its texture, and her heart went wild.

"Soft," he murmured. "Soft, like your mouth." He stared at her lower lip for a long moment. "I'd like to kiss you when I was sober," he said under his breath, "just to see how it would feel."

Her fingers trembled, and he felt it. His hand contracted and brought hers to his mouth. "You smell of perfume," he breathed huskily. "And you go to my head like whiskey when you look at me that way."

She tried to draw her hand back, but he wouldn't let go of it.

"You said you'd teach me," he reminded her with a slow smile. "I'm just getting in some practice."

"I said I'd teach you manners," she replied in a high-pitched tone. "You don't threaten maître d's and waiters and yell across classy restaurants, Carson."

"Okay," he said, smoothing the backs of her fingers against his hard cheek. "What else shouldn't I do?"

"What you're doing right now," she whispered.

"I'm only holding your hand," he said reasonably.

But it didn't feel that way. It felt as if he were reaching over the table and taking possession of her, total and absolute possession of her mind and her heart and even her body.

"Mandelyn," he whispered, as if he were savoring the very sound of her name, and she realized with a start that he'd hardly ever said it. It was usually some casual endearment when he spoke to her. He made her name sound new and sweet.

She watched his dark head bend over her hand with wonder, watched his chiseled lips touch it, brush it with a tenderness she hadn't imagined him capable of. Her breath caught in her throat and tremors like the harbingers of an earthquake began deep in her body.

"Carson?" she whispered back.

His eyes lifted, as if he'd heard something in her voice that he wasn't expecting.

But before he could say anything, the waiter was back with the coffee.

"Where are my crepes?" Carson asked curtly.

"It will be only a minute, monsieur, just a minute," Henri promised with a worried smile and a fervent glance toward the kitchen.

Carson stared after him. "It had better be," he said.

Henri retreated, and Mandelyn had to smother a grin. "You do come on strong, don't you?" she managed with a straight face.

"I learned early that it was the only way to come out on top," he returned. "I don't like being put down. Never did."

"They aren't trying to put you down," she began.

"Like hell," he said, smiling coldly.

She moved restlessly in her chair. "Life-styles among the well-to-do are different."

"You and I are pretty far apart, aren't we?" he asked quietly.

"Oh, I don't know," she murmured. "I used to think I'd enjoy going fishing once in a while, in a pair of old dungarees and a worn-out shirt."

"Did you? I could take you fishing sometime, if you like."

She looked up, half amused, and it dawned on her that she hadn't ever seen him smile as much as he had this one day. "Could you?"

He let his eyes run slowly over her. "I could loan you some old jeans and a shirt, too." He leaned back and lit a cigarette. "After all, you ought to get something out of this deal. You teach me what I need to know. And then I'll teach you a few things." He was looking straight at her when he said it, and she tingled all over.

Henri came back with the crepes seconds later, and Mandelyn was able to damp down her suddenly intense awareness of Carson while she instructed him in the use of flatware.

"Why don't they just give you a fork and let it go at that?" he grumbled when she'd explained the formal arrangement of knife, forks and spoons.

"Because it's etiquette," she told him. "Besides, you can't very well eat soup without a soup spoon, or sweeten tea without a teaspoon, or..."

"I get the idea," he sighed. "I suppose

you'd never forgive me for eating peas on my knife.'

She laughed softly. "I think you might make a record book or two for managing that."

"It's easy," he returned. "All you have to do is get mashed potatoes on the knife and dip it in the peas."

She burst out laughing at the mischief in his eyes. "I give up."

"Not yet, you don't. Eat your crepes. You could use a few extra pounds. You're too thin."

Her eyebrows arched. "I never would have expected you to notice something like that."

He didn't smile. "I notice a hell of a lot about you, Mandelyn."

Once again, the way he said her name made her head swim, and she actually blushed. Her gaze fell back to her plate while Carson slowly cut his crepes.

Minutes later, after a companionable silence and a second cup of coffee, they sampled the restaurant's strawberry crepes.

Mandelyn licked whipped cream from her upper lip and Carson watched the action with an expression she didn't understand. She lifted her eyes to his and felt tremors along her spine.

"It's sexy, don't you know?" he said under his breath as he read the question in her eyes.

"Eating whipped cream?" she laughed nervously, deliberately misunderstanding him.

"Don't play dumb. You know exactly what I mean."

She ignored him and her quickened heartbeat, and finished her crepe.

"How about a movie before we go back to Sweetwater?" he asked.

"Sorry," she laughed. "I have some paperwork to do before I go to bed."

He didn't like that. His eyes glittered across the table at her. "Do you work all the time?"

"Don't you?" she returned. "I can't remember a time in the past few years when you actually took a vacation."

"Vacations are for rich men," he said, dropping his eyes to his coffee cup. He toyed with it idly. "Maybe everyone's right. Maybe I'm not cut out to be a rancher."

"What else could you be?" she teased.

"What do you mean, that I'm too crude and stupid to be anything but a cattleman?" he asked coldly. His voice carried so that people at the other tables immediately looked to see if he fit his own description of himself.

"That's not what I meant at all, and will you please lower your voice?" she asked in a squeaky tone.

"Why should I?" he asked curtly. He threw his napkin down on the table and stood up, glaring around him. "And what are you people staring at?" he asked haughtily. "Who wrote the rules and said that you have to keep your eyes down and speak in whispers and never do anything out of the ordinary in a snobby restaurant? Do you think the waiters here drive Lincolns—is that why you're so afraid of them? Do you think that head waiter has a villa on the Riviera and owns stock in AT&T?" He laughed coldly while Mandelyn seriously considered hiding under the tablecloth. "These people that wait on you are no better or worse than any of you, and you're paying to be here just like I am, so why are you all letting these stuck-up dudes push you around?"

The cattleman a few tables over who was a friend of Carson's burst out laughing.

"Hell, yes, why are we?" he burst out, grinning. "You tell 'em, Carson!"

A lady closer to their table glared at Carson. "It's amazing the kind of people they allow in these restaurants," she said with hauteur.

Carson glared back at her. "Yes, isn't it?" he agreed with a speaking glance. "And it's amazing how many people think they're better than other people because of what they've got, right, lady?"

The lady in question turned red, got up and left.

"Please sit down," Mandelyn pleaded with Carson.

"You sit. I'm leaving. If you're coming with me, come on. And where the hell is the check?" he demanded of a trembling Henri. "I want it now, not when you get around to it."

Henri was writing it as he came, his hand shaking. "Here, monsieur!"

Carson took it and stormed out toward the cashier, leaving Mandelyn to fend for herself. She got up quietly and walked slowly out of the dining room, her poised serenity drawing reluctant admiration. She was Miss Bush of Charleston from her head to her toes.

But serene was the last thing she felt when she caught up with Carson in the parking lot.

"You hot-tempered, ill-mannered, over-bearing son of Satan," she began, her small fists clenched at her sides, her eyes throwing off silvery sparks, her hair glinting with blonde fire in the sunlight.

"Flattery won't work with me," he assured her, grinning at her display of temper.

"Get in, firecracker, and I'll take you home."

"I've never been so embarrassed...!" she began.

"Why?"

"Why!"

He stared at her as she stood rigidly beside the car, not opening her door. "Well, get in," he repeated.

"When you open the door for me," she said icily. "Women's lib or not, it is good manners."

With a resigned sigh, he went around and made an elaborate production of opening the door, helping her inside the car and closing it again.

"I'll never go anywhere with you again as long as I live," she fumed when he'd climbed in beside her and turned the key in the ignition.

"You started it," he reminded her as he pulled out onto the highway. "Making that crack about my ignorance..."

"I did no such thing," she shot back. "I simply asked what else you'd do. You love cattle, you always have. You'd be miserable in any other job and you know it.'

"You meant that I wasn't capable of doing anything else," he returned, his eyes growing fiery again.

"I can't talk to you!" she ground out. "You're always on the defensive with me, you take everything I say the wrong way!"

"I'm a savage, remember?" he asked mockingly. "What else do you expect?"

"God knows," she said. She turned her eyes out the window to the long, arid stretch of land that stretched toward the horizon. "None of this was my idea," she reminded him. "I don't care if you eat peas off your knife for the rest of your life."

There was a long, pregnant silence. He lit a cigarette and smoked it quietly as the miles went by. Eventually, she glanced at him. His face was rigid, his eyes staring straight ahead. He looked unhappy. And she felt guilty about that, guilty about losing her temper. He wanted Patty, and without some polishing, he'd never get her. He must know that and the knowledge was eating him alive.

"How far did you get in school?" she asked suddenly.

He took a deep, slow breath, and wouldn't look at her. "I have a bachelor's degree in business administration, with a minor in economics."

She felt shocked, and it showed.

"I got my education while I was in military service, in the Marines," he told her bluntly. "But that was a long time ago. I've lived hard and I've worked hard and I haven't had time for socializing. I hate pretense. I hate people lying to each other and cutting at each other and pretending to be things they aren't. Most of all," he added hotly, "I hate places that put you down on the basis of your bank account. God, how I hate it!"

He must have spent a good part of his youth being looked down on, humiliated. Her heart thawed. She reached out and touched his sleeve very gently, and he tensed even at that light touch.

"I'm sorry," she said. "Sorry that I lost my temper, that I yelled at you."

"I have scars," he said quietly. "They don't show, and I try to forget them. But they're pretty deep."

She dropped her eyes to his stubborn, square chin. "Still want to take me fishing?"

"I reckon."

"How about Monday?"

He hesitated, and her eyes came up.

"You work on Monday," he reminded her, and there was a strangely puzzled look about him, as if he hadn't expected her to take him seriously.

"So I'll play hookey." She grinned.

He laughed softly. "All right. So will I."

She settled her head back against the seat with a sigh. "If you'll put the worm on the hook," she added. "I'm not committing homicide on any helpless worms."

Later, she thought about that sudden decision to take a day off—something she never did—and go fishing with Carson, of all people. How odd that he'd never mentioned that business degree he held, almost as if he was ashamed of it. She felt vaguely sorry for him. Carson wasn't a bad man. He had wonderful qualities. He'd stayed two nights with old Ben Hamm and his wife on their ranch when the couple had the flu. He'd fed them and taken care of them, and then paid their utility bills for the month because Ben had been unable to work for a week and had gotten behind. Then there was the poor family that he'd "adopted" for Christmas. He'd bought toys for the kids and had a huge turkey with all the trimmings delivered to their home. Yes, Carson was a caring man. He just had an extremely hard shell, and Mandelyn decided that he probably had plenty of reasons for it. What would it be like to know the man beneath the shell? She fell asleep on the thought.

Chapter Four

Bright and early Monday morning she called Angie at home and told her she wasn't coming in to the office.

"I'm going fishing. I'll call in later to see if there are any messages," she told the younger woman.

"Fishing?" Angie burst out.

"Why not?' she replied.

"Excuse me, Miss Bush." Angie cleared her throat. "It's just that I never thought you'd like fishing."

"Well, we'll both find out after this morning. Have a good day."

"You, too."

Mandelyn didn't own a pair of old jeans. She wore a slightly worn pair of designer jeans with a colorful striped pullover shirt and sneakers, and left her hair long. She looked a little less proper than usual, she decided finally.

Carson wasn't outside when she drove up, and she hesitated at the front door when he called for her to come inside. It was a little unnerving to be totally alone with him, but she chided herself for her continuing feeling of uneasiness with him and went inside anyway.

"Just be a minute," he called from the back of the house. The bedrooms must be located there, but she'd never seen them.

"Take your time," she replied. She sighed over the worn furniture and bare walls. With a little paint and love, this house had great possibilities. It wasn't all that old, and it was built sturdily. She pursed her lips, studying it. The room was big, but it could be comfortable, and there was a huge rock fireplace that would be a showpiece with a little cleaning up. The windows were long and elegant, and the floor would have a beauty all its own if it were varnished.

"You won't find any sidewinders under the rug, if that's what you're looking for," Carson taunted from the doorway.

She turned and had to force herself to look away again. He'd obviously just come from a shower. He was fully dressed except for the shirt he was shrugging into, a blue printed one that matched his eyes. She got a wildly exciting glimpse of broad, tanned muscles and a thick pelt of hair running down past the buckled belt around his lean hips, and her heart started beating unexpectedly hard. She'd seen Carson without a shirt before, for God's sake, she told herself, why was it affecting her this way all of a sudden?

"You look elegant even in jeans," he murmured drily. "Couldn't you find anything worn?"

"This is worn." She pouted, turning to find him closer than she'd expected. She took a slow breath and inhaled the scent of a men's cologne that was one of her particular favorites. "You smell good," she blurted out.

"Do I?" He laughed softly.

His hands had stilled on the top buttons of the shirt and he looked down at her in a way that threatened and excited all at the same time. His chiseled mouth was smiling in a faint, sexy way and his blue eyes narrowed as they studied her.

"Why are you so nervous?" he asked with his head lifted, so that he was looking down his crooked nose at her. "You've been alone with me before."

"You were always dressed before," she said without meaning to.

"Is that it?" He watched her face and deliberately flicked open the buttons he'd fastened. "Does this bother you?" he asked in a deep, lazy tone, moving the shirt aside to let the hair-roughened expanse of his chest show.

Her breath caught and she didn't understand why. Her lips went dry, but she barely noticed.

He lifted her hands with slow, easy movements, and brought her fingers to his cool skin, letting her feel the hard muscles.

"No flab," she laughed unsteadily, trying to keep things light between them, but her legs felt shaky.

"Not a bit," he agreed. "I work too hard for that." He pressed her fingers hard against him and moved them in a slow, sensuous pattern down the center of his chest and back up again. "I don't suppose you brought a fishing pole?"

"I don't...own one," she replied. Incredible, that they were conducting an impersonal conversation while what they were doing was growing quickly more intimate.

His chest rose and fell unevenly. He pressed her palms flat against his hardened nipples and she could hear his heartbeat, actually hear it. He moved, so that he was closer than ever, and his breath stirred the hair at her temples.

She couldn't look up, because she wanted his mouth desperately, and she knew he'd see it. She didn't understand her own wild hungers or his unexpected reaction to her nearness and her touch. She didn't understand anything.

The room seemed dark and private. There was no sound in it, except for his breathing and the loud tick of the mantel clock.

He drew his open mouth tenderly across her forehead, his breath hot, his chest shuddering with the harshness of his breathing. Impatiently, he took her hands in his and guided them down the hard muscles of his chest and around to his lean hips. She protested, a stiff little gesture.

"Don't fight me," he whispered unsteadily, moving her hands down the sides of his legs and back up to his hips. "There's nothing to be afraid of."

But there was! Her own reaction to him was terrifying. She felt his legs touch hers and she made an odd sound in her throat, one that he heard.

His head moved nearer. Her eyes closed and she felt his warm breath at her forehead, her nose, the open softness of her mouth. Unaware of her response, she opened her mouth to invite his, tilted her head back to give him full access. And waited, breathing in his scent as his mouth came closer. Would it be gentle this time, she wondered, or would he hurt...?

"Mr. Wayne!" The loud call was like a gunshot. Carson's head jerked up. He looked dazed, and his eyes were a dark blue, haunted, hungry as they met hers for just an instant before he moved away.

"What is it, Jake?" he asked curtly, buttoning his shirt as he went out onto the porch.

Mandelyn heard the voices with a sense of unreality. She was still trembling, and her mouth was hungry for the kiss she hadn't gotten. Her misty eyes searched for Carson and found him standing outside the door. She looked at him with open wonder, letting her rapt eyes wander down the superb masculinity of his back and hips and legs. She remembered the feel of his skin, the smell of him. Her breasts ached and as she crossed her arms, she felt the nipples' hardness.

She licked her dry lips and ground her teeth together as she tried to get her rebellious body back under control. It wanted him. God, it wanted him, all of him, skin against skin, mouth against hungry mouth. She almost moaned aloud at the force of that wanting, at the urgency she'd never felt before. Her sweet memories of the man in her past had faded completely away during that passionate onslaught, had been replaced with a different emotion. With a wildness that she'd never known, a violent need.

How in the world could she face Carson now, after giving herself away so completely? He was still a man, he wouldn't hesitate to take anything that was offered, despite their long friendship. If she acted like a temptress, what could she expect? He was human.

She cleared her throat as he came back into the room. If only she could find an excuse to go home.

"I'll find you a pole," he said good-humoredly, grinning at her. "Got a hat?"

"No."

"Here." He reached into the closet and tossed her a straw one that just fit. "It belonged to me, years back. Well, let's go."

He herded her out the door before she had a chance to protest, and minutes later they went bumping over his pasture in the pickup truck toward the stream where the swimming and fishing hole spread out invitingly past some cottonwood trees.

"We used to swim here," he told her as they sat on upside-down minnow buckets in the cool shade. "Some of the boys still do, but it's a good fishing spot, nevertheless. Here."

He handed her the bait can and she stared at it distastefully.

"Please?" she asked softly, looking up at him.

His eyes remained on hers for a minute before he turned them back to the bait can. "I'll show you how."

"But, Carson..."

"Just watch."

He threaded worms onto the hook while she grimaced. "Soft-hearted little thing," he chided. "I'll never take you rabbit hunting, that's for sure."

She stuck out her tongue at him. "Well, I wouldn't go, so don't ask me."

"Patty's having a party next Friday night," he said as he threw her line into the stream. The red cork bobbed gaily against the murky water. He glanced at her.

"Is she?" she asked in a breathless tone.

He threaded worms onto his own hook. "Kind of a social gathering, I think, so folks can get acquainted with her and tour her new office."

"She's really proud of it," she murmured.

He threw his own line in and leaned his elbows on his knees, holding the pole between them. Nearby birds were calling, and crickets made pleasant sounds in the underbrush.

She glanced at him. "Are you going?"

He laughed shortly. "You know I don't socialize."

She looked down at the ground. "I could . . . teach you."

His eyes glanced sideways. "Could you?"

"You've got the clothes now," she reminded him. "All you need to know is some of the new dance steps and how to talk to people."

He stared at her for a long moment. "Yes."

She shifted on the bucket. "Well, do you want to?"

"Want to what?" he asked huskily.

She looked up into his eyes and felt herself going hot all over. She dragged her gaze back to the water. "Uh, do you want me to teach you?"

"I think you may be the one who needs teaching," he said.

Her face flamed, because she knew exactly what he was talking about. She felt like a girl on her first date, tongue-tied and expectant.

"I know how to dance," she said.

"Deliberately misunderstanding me again?" he said with a soft laugh.

"I thought we came here to fish?"

"I am."

"Do you want to learn to dance or not?" she asked impatiently.

"I guess so."

"You can come over tomorrow night, if you want to," she said. "I'll make supper."

He studied her for a long moment. "All right."

She tingled from head to toe in a new, exciting way. She smiled, and he watched the movement of her lips with an expression that it was just as well she didn't see. It would have frightened her.

She studied the bobbing red cork with drowsy, contented eyes, hardly aware when it went straight under. When she felt the tug on the line and realized what was happening, she jerked too soon. The hook came flying up on the bank, straight into her shirt and caught there.

"My God, were you trying to send the fish to the moon?" Carson drawled. "You caught something at least."

She glared at him. "My favorite shirt," she moaned, letting her eyes fall to the hook sticking through the soft fabric just above the peak of her tiptilted breast.

"Hold still and I'll get it out for you," he said. He put down his pole and knelt beside her.

She hadn't realized how intimate it was going to be. In order to extricate the barbed hook, he had to slide one lean, work-roughened hand into the vee-neck of the shirt. And Mandelyn wasn't wearing a bra. That discovery made Carson start violently.

His eyes met hers. She could see the dark blue circles around his lighter blue irises, and the black thickness of his lashes. But what she was feeling was the touch of his knuckles on her bare breast, and her body was reacting noticeably to it.

"Carson, I can get it out," she said too quickly.

"Let me," he whispered. But he was holding her eyes when he said it, and his fingers were moving very delicately on bare skin. She trembled.

He smelled of wind and fir trees and desert. And his skin was rough against her softness, but it was a natural roughness, like sand against silk, or bark against water.

Even the crickets seemed to have gone mute. There was silence all around them in the little glade. Nothing existed except Mandelyn's awed face and Carson's hard one, and the sound of his breathing as he closed his eyes and tenderly cradled Mandelyn's head in one big hand.

She jerked a little in reaction, but he shook his head slowly and lowered his face toward her.

"Sit still, Mandy," he whispered as his lips stroked her mouth. "I just want to see how you taste when I'm sober."

"Carson, your hand..." she whispered half-heartedly, and her slender fingers touched his hairy wrist in token protest.

"Shh," he breathed. His mouth was like a teasing breeze, brushing at her lips. His fingers stroked over the soft curve of her breast, edging toward the hard tip with every movement, teasing her body as he teased her mouth.

She stiffened, moved. Her eyes opened, her breath quickened. His face was so close that all she could see was his mouth. He'd shaved. That registered. And he tasted of smoke and coffee and mint. But his hand...!

She caught it just as his thumb and forefinger found the hard tip, and her nails bit into him helplessly and she moaned. It took every ounce of will power she had to move his hand away. She was afraid of the new sensations she was feeling. She was afraid of Carson.

"All right," he said softly, not offended at all. Her flushed face and wide, frightened eyes told him everything he needed to know. His hand brushed the long strands of hair away from her cheeks, and he looked at her with such reverence that she couldn't seem to move.

"The hook," she reminded him.

"Yes," he murmured, smiling faintly. "Later. I want that kiss, honey."

Her heart was beating so wildly that she could barely breathe at all. His head bent and she waited for his mouth, no protest left in her, only a sense of anticipation.

His lips were warm and hard and exquisitely tender. She closed her eyes with a soft sigh and let him do what he wanted. He eased between her trembling lips, letting her feel the texture of his own. Her hands dug into the hard muscles of his shoulders in an agony of wanting.

But still he teased her, rubbing his closed lips between her open ones, nibbling at her soft mouth. And then he stopped. She moaned aloud as he got to his feet and reached down to bring her body into the hard curve of his.

"It's all right," he murmured, wrapping her securely in his arms. "I only want to feel you while we kiss."

She reached up, hesitant, and touched his hard face.

"Carson," she whispered.

His chest rose and fell roughly. "I've waited years for you to say my name that way," he murmured unsteadily as he bent again. "Years, centuries..."

"Hard," she pleaded, trembling. "Hard, please . . . !"

A tremor ran through him, probably of shock, she thought dizzily as he took her open mouth. She'd shocked herself with the whispered demand. She tasted him, experienced him with every sense she had as he gently crushed her breasts into his hard chest and his mouth merged roughly, intimately with her own. His tongue stabbed between her teeth, into the dark warmth of her mouth, tangling with her tongue in a wild, exquisite exploration.

He groaned against her mouth. A faint tremor shook his arms, and she arched into his body. She wanted him. Her body told her that, it screamed at her to end this sweet torment. She wanted to feel his skin against hers, she wanted the driving power of his body to overwhelm her, possess her. She wanted his open mouth on her soft breasts. . . .

When he lifted his head abruptly, it was like being thrown to the ground. She shivered.

His darkened blue eyes searched hers quickly, intensely, and although he'd loosened his grip, he still held her by the arms. He started to draw back and her shirt came with him.

"Oh, hell," he muttered, looking down. The hook that had gone through her blouse had caught in the thick pocket of his shirt.

She started laughing as reaction set in. Her twinkling eyes sought his. "I've hooked you," she teased.

He stared at her for a long moment. "I haven't seen you laugh before. Not like this."

"I haven't felt like this before," she blurted out. "I mean, being relaxed and going fishing and . . . and being myself."

"Stand still while I get us untangled," he said, and reached down, frowning as he tried to extract the barbed end of the hook from his pocket. "Damn, I'll have to cut it," he muttered. He dove into his pocket and dragged out an old pocket knife, expertly extracting the blade and slicing deftly through the fabric. His eyes glanced at her apologetically. "Sorry, honey, but this is the only way. I'll buy you another blouse."

"You don't have to do that. It was my fault, after all," she said breathlessly.

"Stand still, so I don't nick you," he said softly and slid his hand under the fabric again, against her bare skin.

She felt wildly female at the feel and sight of that dark-skinned, tough hand inside her blouse. Her lips parted and she studied the face so close to hers with wide, fascinated eyes.

He felt the stare and looked down into her eyes. His hands paused in their task and he watched her for a long moment. "Why didn't you want me to touch you?" he whispered.

Her lower lip trembled a little. "I... haven't been touched ... that way since I was eighteen, Carson," she said unsteadily.

"If I'd persisted a minute longer, you'd have let me, though, wouldn't you?" he asked.

She licked her dry lips and her wide gray eyes searched his blue ones with uncertainty. "I didn't expect that," she whispered.

"Why not? I'm human, Mandy. I may be rough and half-civilized, but I'm capable of wanting a woman."

"Oh, I didn't mean it like that," she said, touching his hard mouth with her fingers. She searched his eyes curiously. "Carson...you...you've had women, haven't you?"

Time seemed to hang suspended between them. "Yes," he said quietly.

Her breath shuddered out of her throat. Her fingers traced his lips unsteadily, with helpless pleasure. "I've never been to bed with a man," she breathed.

His nostrils flared. His chest rose and fell raggedly. "You're twenty-six."

She smiled nervously. Having him this close was affecting her wildly. "Yes, I know. Do you think I might get in the record books?"

"Not," he sighed heavily, "if you keep touching me that way."

"Oh!" Belatedly she realized just how intimate her fingers had grown on his face. She moved them back down to his arm. "Sorry."

"You excite me," he admitted, turning his attention back to the hook. He sliced the fabric gently, not unaware of her hot blush or the increasing pressure of her fingers. "So watch out."

That wasn't going to be easy, she realized, feeling his warm fingers being slowly removed from her blouse. "Thank you," she said as he removed the hook as well.

"My pleasure," he murmured drily.

"Carson, I didn't mean to..." she began, losing her train of thought when he looked down into her eyes. "I didn't know...I wasn't..."

"Hush." He handed her the fishing pole with a warm, knowing look. "I haven't been with a woman in a long time," he said slowly. "It was a moment out of time, that's all. Nothing to be afraid of."

"Of course." She managed to get a worm on the hook and began talking real estate, out of nervousness. She'd reacted to Carson's lovemaking like a shy young girl, and she knew now that while he might need lessons in deportment, he'd never need them as a lover. He knew exactly what to do with a woman. And now she was more afraid of him than ever. In all the years she'd known him, she'd never thought of him as a lover. Now it was impossible to think of him any other way.

He followed her lead in conversation, and they talked about general things for a long time while the day moved lazily by. After they had caught a good number of fish, they packed up their gear and went back to the house.

"I've enjoyed today. Thank you," she said. She was reluctant to leave him, and that was odd. In the past she'd always been glad to get out of his sight.

"So have I," he replied. He studied her for a long moment. "Want to stay for supper? We can cook the fish together."

She should have said no. But she didn't. Her face lit up and she smiled. "Sure!"

He chuckled. "Want to clean them for me?"

She frowned. "Carson, I hate to be a drag, but I don't think I know how. Uncle didn't fish, you know."

"Yes, and cleaning fish isn't something you learn in finishing school, is it, little lady?"

He didn't say it in an insulting way. She searched his hard face. "Does it bother you, my background?"

"No," he said firmly. "If you want to know, I think a lot of you. Until you came along, I'd never met a real lady."

"You wouldn't think I was one at times, though," she murmured, smiling at him as she followed him into the kitchen.

"You're a firecracker sometimes, all right," he agreed. He caught her by the waist after he'd put down the string of fish, and jerked her against his body. "But I like you that way, Mandy. A woman with a temper," he murmured, bending, "is usually pretty passionate...."

His mouth crushed down against hers and she moaned, the sound unusually loud in the confines of the room as she savored his strength, the urgency of his hard kiss.

He lifted his head, his eyes glittering with some new emotion. "Why did you moan?" he asked roughly. "Fear or pleasure?"

Her lips trembled and, embarrassed, she pulled away. "I'll get started on the fish."

He watched her for a minute speculatively and then he smiled. "I'll get some potatoes to fry."

It was a quiet supper. She enjoyed her crisp fish, but Carson seemed preoccupied.

"Want to call it off?" she asked.

His head came up. "What?"

"Tomorrow night."

He shook his head. "No. I want to learn to dance." His eyes dropped to her soft mouth. "With you," he added softly.

Her chest felt tight. He was doing it again, using that wicked charm that she hadn't known he possessed.

"I have to practice on somebody, don't I?" he asked when he saw her hesitation. "I thought teaching me how to make love went part and parcel with teaching me to court a woman," he added with a wicked smile.

She flushed. "You don't need teaching in that department, and well you know it," she said.

His eyebrows arched. "I don't?"

She looked up. Her wide eyes pleaded with him. "Don't take advantage, will you?" she asked softly. "I'm afraid of you, a little."

"Yes, I know you are," he replied, his voice deep and quiet in the stillness of the room. He reached across the table and took her small hand in his, rubbing his thumb over the silky skin. "Haven't you ever wanted a man, or was it that exclusive upbringing that kept you innocent?"

"That exclusive upbringing is the downfall of a lot of girls," she murmured drily. "Most of the others were quite experienced."

"Didn't you date?"

That brought back painful memories, and she didn't want to face them. She shrugged.

"I was terribly shy in those days. It was hard for me to talk to men at all."

"Not when you got out here," he chuckled. "I'll never forget the first time I saw you."

"I slapped you," she recalled with a wicked smile. "I didn't know at the time how dangerous that was."

"I would never hit you back," he said. "I'd cut off my arm first."

"That's what Jake knows, that's why I always get rousted out of bed to come and save the world from you," she laughed.

He studied her hand. "Jake isn't as blind as you are, I guess."

"Blind?"

"It doesn't matter." He let go of her fingers and lit a cigarette. His eyes searched hers. "Getting dark. You'd better go home, before somebody makes a remark about your being here alone with me after dark."

"Would that bother you?"

"Yes," he said simply. "I don't want any blemish on your reputation. I'd fire any one of my men who suggested that anything improper went on here.''

"It did this afternoon," she blurted out and then flushed.

He searched her eyes slowly. "I wanted to see if I could make you want me," he explained quietly.

She got up from the table in such a rush that she almost knocked over her chair. "I'd better go," she faltered.

He got up, too, and walked along behind her at a slow, steady, confident pace.

"Was that too crude a remark for a gentleman to make?" he murmured drily. "Sorry, Mandy, I don't always think before I say things to you. Look on it as getting some sexual experience. You seem to be pretty backward yourself in that department."

She turned at the front porch and met his stare levelly. "Are you sorry? Would you rather I was experienced?"

He reached out and put his knuckles against her lips. "I'd like, very much, to let you get that kind of experience with me," he said quietly. "Because the way I'd take you, even the first time would be good. I'd make sure of it."

She could hardly walk, her knees felt so weak. She headed for her car in a daze, wondering at the explosive quality of their changing relationship.

"Hey," he called as she opened her car door.

"What?" she asked.

"What time tomorrow night?"

She swallowed and looked back. He was standing on the porch, leaning against a post. The soft light of the kerosene lanterns outlined his superb physique. He looked devastating, and she wondered what he'd do if she walked back up on that porch and kissed him.

"Oh . . . about six," she faltered.

"Do I dress?"

"You'd better," she said, "if we're going to do the thing properly."

"By all means," he murmured drily. " 'Night, honey."

"Good night, Carson."

She drove off, jerking the car as she never had before. Carson was getting to her! She must be off her rocker to let him get under her skin that way. She was the teacher, not Carson. At least, it had started out that way. She had to be careful. Her memories of love were too sweet to let reality interfere with them. She'd learned the hard way that loving was the first step to agony. She didn't want to go through it again. She couldn't! From now on, she'd just keep Carson at arm's length. It was safer that way.

Chapter Five

Mandelyn went home and paced the floor until bedtime. And then she tossed and turned for hours, remembering vividly the touch of Carson's lean fingers on her breast, the fierce hunger of his mouth on her own. She felt on fire for him, and part of her hated the reaction.

It had been years. Years, since she'd felt passion. She hadn't wanted to give herself over to it again, and yet Carson had kindled an emotion in her that overwhelmed her tenderest memories of the past. She'd never felt so violent, so hungry. She rolled over onto her back and stared at the ceiling. Perhaps it was her age. Perhaps she'd reached the brink of spinsterhood and was feeling alone, as Carson felt alone.

She could picture him, blue eyes devouring her face, dark-skinned hands so gentle on her body....

Of course, it could just be infatuation. He was her creation, after all, she was teaching him. Yes, that could be it. She could be like Svengali, overcome by pride. But if that was it, why did she tingle when she thought about Carson? She closed her eyes and thought about birds.

Patty came by the office the next day at lunchtime with some documents from the bank. "Here are the loan papers," she said with a grin. "What time do we meet with that attorney?"

"Today at five," Mandelyn said. "Happy?"

"Just ecstatic," came the reply. "I've got to run out to Carson's and see about that bull. Want to come along, and we'll swing by the barbecue place and have lunch on the way back?''

"Yes, I'd like that," Mandelyn said. "Angie, just close up at noon when you get your own lunch, okay?''

Angie nodded. "Have fun.''

Fun! Mandelyn's heart was racing wildly as she climbed into the red pickup truck beside Patty. She didn't really want to see Carson, but he was coming to her house for dinner that night so she couldn't very well avoid him.

Carson wasn't at the house when they drove up. The door was closed and locked.

"I wonder where he could be?" Patty asked, nibbling on her lip. "Surely to goodness he knew I was coming?''

"Maybe he's in the barn," Mandelyn suggested.

Patty sighed. "Boy, am I sharp, not to have thought of that. Maybe I should try another profession . . . yep, look, there's the ranch pickup.''

They walked down to the barn. Mandelyn wished she hadn't worn the spiked high heels that went so well with her jaunty little two-piece blue and white suite. But when she entered the barn and saw the frank appreciation on Carson's face, she decided it was worth a little discomfort. He was half kneeling beside his bull, with Jake at his side, and he couldn't seem to take his eyes off her.

Both men got to their feet, and Mandelyn couldn't help noticing how animated Patty suddenly became. She was wearing jeans and a tee shirt, and had her hair pulled back in a bun, but she still looked feminine and cute, and Carson gave her a big grin and hugged her.

"There's my best girl," he said, and Mandelyn felt suddenly murderous.

"How's my patient?" Patty asked, hugging him back while Jake looked at them with an expression Mandelyn couldn't quite describe.

"Well, he's about the same," Carson sighed, staring down at the bull. He still had an arm around Patty, and Mandelyn found she resented it.

Patty got down beside the big animal, a Hereford, and checked him over with professional thoroughness. "We'll try another dose of the same, and see if that won't do it. He's improved some, Carson, I think we can save him."

"If you don't, I may never speak to you again," Carson assured her. "And I'll guarantee at least five of my cows will die of broken hearts, judging by the way they've behaved since he's been out of action."

Mandelyn flushed, but Patty only laughed. "We'll restore him to his former vigor. Let me get my bag. Mandy, you aren't in a rush to get back, are you?"

"No," came the quiet reply. "I don't have anything pressing."

"Here, I'll help with that bag," Jake said curtly, and walked out of the barn behind Patty with a determined stride. Mandelyn had never actually seen the easygoing foreman move so quickly.

Carson studied Mandelyn with narrow, thoughtful eyes, hands on his hips, powerful legs apart. "You're quiet. And you won't look at me. Why?"

Her eyes glanced off his and back down to the bull. "What's the matter with the bull?" she asked nervously.

He moved closer, ignoring the question. So close that she could smell him, feel him, touch him if she chose. His shirt was half unbuttoned, and she wanted to reach out and rip it open....

His fingers tilted her oval face up to his eyes, and he looked at her for a long time. "Shy, Mandy?" he asked softly.

She flushed and tried to look away, but he wouldn't let her. Her lips parted on a rush of breath.

"Tonight," he whispered, making a promise of it as he searched her wide eyes.

Her lips trembled and he started to bend toward them, his eyes intent, his lean hand moving to the back of her head to position her face where he wanted it. And just as his open mouth started to touch hers, the truck door slammed.

He laughed. "I seem to spend my life trying to kiss you without interruptions, don't I, honey?"

She managed a nervous laugh, too, but her eyes were wary. She didn't miss the speculative look he sent toward Patty and Jake, or the way he moved quickly back to his bull. Was he trying to make the other girl jealous?

She didn't say another word until Patty was ready to go, and then she all but ran for the truck. Carson made her nervous, he intimidated her. She sat there listening as Patty told him what else to do for the sick bull. And all the while Mandelyn never actually looked at him. She was frightened of what her eyes might tell him.

"You sure were quiet today," Patty remarked as they ate a hamburger at a local restaurant known for its barbecue. "You and Carson have a fight or something?"

"Oh, nothing like that," Mandelyn said. "We, uh, I just couldn't think of anything to say, that's all. I don't know a lot about animals."

"I love them," Patty sighed. "I always did. There was never anything I wanted to be more than a vet." She glanced suspiciously at Mandelyn. "What was going on in the barn when Jake and I walked in, by the way? You were hot and bothered like I've never seen you. Carson make a pass?"

"You know I don't feel that way about Carson," Mandelyn said nervously, making a jerking motion with her hand that knocked over her cup of soda.

Patty ran for more napkins, and Mandelyn sat there in the ruin of her suit wondering if it would be undignified to scream.

The rest of the day was no better. She didn't make a single sale, although she did show one undecided young couple six houses only to learn that at least one major thing was wrong with each. She stopped by the attorney's office for the closing on Patty's new building, and then locked up her own office with a weary sigh. She still had to think of something to fix for supper. And Carson was coming!

She jumped in her car and made a wild rush home to see what she had to cook. Thank goodness there was some chicken she could fry and some vegetables. She took off her suit, put on jeans and a loose shirt, and got to it. She didn't even think about what lay ahead; it made her too nervous. Things were getting entirely out of hand with him, and she didn't know what to do anymore. What had begun as a simple etiquette course now promised to be a full-fledged affair if she didn't watch her step. It occurred to her that he wanted her, physically. But she knew that he could feel that way and still be in love with Patty. It wasn't the same with men as it was with women. Which made her even more nervous about her own survival instincts. They didn't seem to work with Carson.

Just before six, she tried on five outfits before deciding on a demure little yellow sundress. She left her hair down and brushed it to silky perfection, and then stared at herself in the mirror and hoped she didn't look too eager or too dressed up. She hadn't been so excited in years, and over Carson, of all people!

He got there five minutes early, just as she'd finished dishing up the chicken and vegetables. She ran to the door to let him in, and smiled in helpless appreciation at the way he looked.

He was wearing one of the new outfits they'd bought him—tan slacks with a patterned shirt and a casual white and tan plaid blazer. He was freshly shaven and his hair, under his Stetson, was well-groomed. He smelled of fine cologne and he looked good enough to eat.

"Well?" he asked impatiently.

She stood aside to let him in, sensitive to the sweeping glance he gave her. "You look very nice," she murmured.

"So do you. Good enough to be the main course, in fact."

She grinned. "I'd give you a rash."

"Think so?" He tossed his hat onto the chair and there was a sudden sharp gleam in his eyes.

She knew what he was thinking, and it frightened her. She went hurriedly ahead of him into the dining room, where the table was already laid, including iced tea in tall glasses.

"I'd just finished," she explained. "Shall we start?"

He sighed. "I guess so," he said with a wistful glance in her direction.

She stood by her chair while he sat down and shook out his napkin.

"Ahem!" she cleared her throat.

He glanced up. "Something wrong with your throat?"

"I'm waiting for you to seat me."

"Oh." He got to his feet, frowning. The gleam came back into his blue, blue eyes. He pulled out her chair and bent and lifted her in his hard arms. "Like this?" he asked softly, putting her down in the chair with his mouth hovering just above her own.

"N-not exactly," she whispered back. Her eyes fell to his mouth, and she wanted it. Wanted it . . . !

He seemed to know that, because he straightened with a purely masculine smile on his face and went back to his own chair.

"This looks good," he murmured while she tried to get her heart to settle down, her lungs to work again.

"I hope it tastes that way," she said tautly. "It was a rush job. I had a long afternoon."

"So did I."

"How's your bull?" she asked, handing him the platter of chicken.

"He'll make it. He was better after that second shot. Poor old critter, I felt sorry for him."

"I thought it was the cows you felt sorry for," she murmured demurely.

He studied her downbent head for a long moment before he dished out some mashed potatoes onto his plate. "You ought to come over when I turn him back out into the pasture," he said drily. "You'd learn a few things."

She all but overturned her tea glass, and he threw back his black head and laughed uproariously.

"All right, I give up, you're out of my league," she burst out. "You terrible man!"

"You need to spend some time around Patty," he remarked. "She'd put you on the right track soon enough. A girl after my own heart."

Which was probably true, she thought miserably. Patty would suit him to a tee. He might want Mandelyn, but Patty appealed to his mind and heart. How terrible, to be wanted only for her body.

"You put out salad forks," he remarked. "Why? You didn't make a salad."

"I meant to," she said.

"Etiquette," he scoffed. "I'll be damned if I understand any of it. A bunch of rules and regulations for snobs, if you ask me. Why dress up a table like this when all you do is eat, anyway? Who the hell cares which fork you eat what with?"

"Ladies and gentlemen do," she said, biting down hard on a roll.

"I'm not much of a gentleman, am I?" he sighed. "I don't suppose if I worked at it all my life, I'd improve a hell of a lot."

"Yes, you will," she said softly. She studied his craggy face, liking its hardness, its strength. Her eyes fell to his slender hand and she remembered how tender it had been on her bare skin. She dropped her fork noisily against her plate and scrambled to pick it up.

"Do I make you nervous, Mandelyn?" he murmured wryly. "That's a first."

She shifted in her seat. "I'm not used to entertaining men here," she admitted.

"Yes, I know that."

He was watching her, the way he always did, and that made her more nervous than ever. They finished the meal in silence, and he helped her carry the dishes into the kitchen. Not only that—he insisted on helping as she washed them. He dried them, smiling at her confusion.

"I'm handy in the kitchen," he reminded her. "I have to be or I'd have starved to death years ago. I don't have women over to cook my dinner."

She lifted her eyes to his hard face and searched it curiously.

He looked down at the curious expression on her flushed face. "Yes, once in a while they come over for other purposes," he said softly. "I'm a man, not a plaster saint, and I have all the usual needs."

Her face colored slowly and he grinned. She tore her eyes away, but her hands trembled and she hated that giveaway sign.

"You're such a little greenhorn," he murmured. "You don't know anything about men and women, do you?"

"I'm not ignorant," she muttered.

"I didn't say you were. Just innocent." He finished drying the last dish and put it to one side. "I like that. Your being innocent, I mean. I like it a lot."

She couldn't meet his eyes. He made her feel shy and young and all thumbs.

"Why hasn't there been a man?" he asked quietly.

"Let's start your dancing lessons, shall we?" she began nervously. She started past him, but he caught her.

"Why, Mandelyn?" he persisted.

"Carson . . ."

His big hands caught her waist and crushed her body against his. "Why, damn it?" he burst out, his patience at an end.

Her vulnerability to his nearness shocked her. She panicked and suddenly tore away from him as if she couldn't bear for him to touch her. She stood with her back to him, shivering.

She knew he hadn't liked her withdrawal, not one bit. But she couldn't help it, he terrified her. She was getting in over her head, and she didn't know how to stop him, how to handle him. Carson was more man pound for pound than she'd ever seen.

She swallowed down a rush of shyness and turned back to face him. He was preoccupied, as if he was thinking deep thoughts. He came close again, his gaze intent.

"Suppose you show me how to dance," he said at last. "Then next week comes culture. I've bought tickets for a ballet in Phoenix. I thought you might come along and explain it all to me."

She laughed. "You, at a ballet?"

He glared at her. "Stop that!"

"Yes, Carson," she said demurely.

"Turn on that damned stereo, will you?"

A moment later the music flowed sweetly into the silence. Mandelyn went easily into his arms and showed him how to hold her, not too tightly, not too loosely. Then she taught him what to do with his feet. He was a little clumsy at first, but an apt enough student.

"Why do I have to hold you so far away?" he asked. "I've seen couples practically making love on the dance floor."

"Not in polite company," she said huskily, staring at her feet.

"Yes, in polite company," he murmured. His hands brought her gently closer, until she was standing right up against him, so close that she could feel his heartbeat against her breasts. "Like this. Here." He brought one of her hands up to his neck and slid his arm further around her, resting his chin on her head. "Mmm," he murmured, "much better."

That depended on one's point of view, she thought nervously. She felt stiff, because her body was reacting to his like wildfire.

"Don't panic," he said softly. "We'll just dance."

But she was all too close to him, and something had happened to his body that she'd never experienced before. She tried to edge a little away from him, but he held her fast.

"Carson," she protested weakly.

"Mandelyn, I know you're a virgin," he said quietly. "I'm not going to make a wild grab for you."

"Yes, I know, but . . . but . . ."

"But you can feel me wanting you and you're frightened, isn't that it?" He lifted his head and searched her eyes. "I'm not embarrassed. Why should you be? It's a man's very natural reaction to a lovely woman."

She'd never heard it put like that. She studied his hard face.

"I've spent my life working with animals," he said, his voice quiet, deep. "I don't find anything distasteful about reproduction, about sex. You shouldn't either. It's God's way of perpetuating the species, and it's beautiful.''

She flushed, but she didn't look away. "You make it sound that way," she said softly.

His eyes searched hers intimately. "I don't like the idea of one-night stands and affairs, or people living together without marriage. I'm old-fashioned enough to want a woman with principles when I marry, and not a woman who'll proposition me just because she feels liberated.''

Her eyebrows arched. "Has that ever happened to you?'' she asked.

He laughed softly. "As a matter of fact, yes, at a cattle convention, of all places. She was a little rodeo rider and as pretty as a picture. She came up to me, touched me in a way I won't even tell you about and invited me to spend the night with her.''

She hesitated. "Did you?'' she asked in a tiny voice, all eyes.

He studied her mouth for a long moment. "Shame on you. A well brought up young woman like you, asking a man that kind of question...."

"Did you sleep with her?" she persisted.

"No, as a matter of fact, I didn't," he chuckled. "I like to do the chasing."

"Yes, I imagine you would," she replied, but she felt relieved all the same.

His hand slid down her back to the bottom of her spine and pushed her just a little closer, and she caught her breath and froze.

"Too intimate?" he murmured. "Okay, I get the message. The kind of girls I'm used to don't mind being held like that. But I guess I've got a lot to learn about civilized behavior."

She nuzzled her face against his chest with a sigh. "I've got a lot to learn about the reverse," she said with a smile. "No one's ever held me this way."

His hands contracted on her waist, and she gasped. "Hey, not so tight," she laughed. "That hurts!"

"Why don't you go out with anyone?"

That was a good question, but it wasn't the time for confessions. "I like my own company," she said after a minute.

"You'll need a man one day."

"No," she protested. "I don't want anyone."

His hand caught suddenly in the thick length of her hair and tugged sharply. She gasped at the twinge of pain and stared at him as if he were a stranger.

"You can't live alone forever," he said harshly, his eyes glittering down into hers. "You need more than your work."

"What do I need, since you're such an expert on the subject?" she challenged hotly.

He pulled her hair, more gently now, forcing her head down onto his shoulder while the music played on, forgotten. "You need to be dragged into a man's bed and loved all night long. That's what you need."

"Not with you," she protested, pushing against his hard chest. "You've got a woman already!"

He wouldn't let go. "I have?"

"Of course," she grumbled, pushing harder. "The one we're remodeling you for, remember? The one who's too stuck up to like you the way...you are...will you let go of me, damn it!" She stood still, hating the slow, sweet stirrings of her own body as he held her and she felt his heartbeat merging with her own.

His chest rose and fell with gathering speed, and the hand holding her long hair released it and began a caressing motion.

It dawned on her that the music was still playing, a sultry tune that only made more dangerous an already flammable situation.

"Dance, don't fight," he whispered deeply. "Don't fight me."

Her legs were trembling as he drew her into a rhythm that was more like making love to music than dancing. His hard thighs brushed her own and never in her life had she felt weaker or more vulnerable.

"I'm afraid." She didn't know that she'd said it out loud, or that Carson's pale blue eyes glittered like diamonds when he heard her.

"Yes, I know," he breathed into her hair. His fingers slid between hers caressingly. "I won't hurt you."

Her nails pressed unconsciously against his chest and he stiffened. She frowned, drawing back so that she could see his face. What she found there disturbed her.

His nostrils flared, his jaw clenched. "No, you aren't the only one who's vulnerable," he said curtly.

Her fascinated eyes searched his. Her rebellious hands liked his visible reaction to them. They opened the top button of his shirt, and his breath caught, but he didn't make a move to stop her.

Her lower lip trembled. "I ... Carson?" she whispered questioningly.

"Go ahead," he breathed. "Do it."

"But ..."

His open mouth touched her forehead. "Do it."

He was trembling already. By the time she fumbled open the shirt and eased the edges aside, his quickened breathing was visible as well. Fascinated, she put her hands flat on the hair-roughened flesh and began to caress him with slow, tentative movements. He seemed to like what she was doing, if the intent hardness of his expression was any indication.

She slid her hands around to his muscular back and laid her hot cheek against his bare skin and closed her eyes. He smelled clean and sexy, and she drew her cheek, then her lips, against his body with dreamy motions.

His fingers tangled in her hair and turned her face, so that her mouth was against him.

"Kiss me," he whispered. "No, honey, not like that. Open your mouth and do it. Yes," he groaned unsteadily, and his hands grew rough. "Yes."

She drew her mouth over every hard inch of his chest, up to his shoulders, his throat, his chin. But even on tiptoe, she couldn't reach his mouth.

"Carson," she moaned protestingly, tugging at his thick hair.

"Do you want my mouth?" he whispered.

"Oh, yes," she whispered back. She moved her body against his slowly. "Oh, yes, I want it very, very much!"

He bent and touched her lips with his, savoring them for a few taut seconds until her mouth opened. His arms drew her close, his hand held the back of her head still, and the kiss became explosive and hot. He groaned as he felt her quick, fervent response to it. His hands moved down to her hips and pushed them against his, and this time she didn't protest.

Her hands worshipped him, running hungrily up his spine, to his shoulder blades, around to his hard ribs and, daringly, to the muscular stomach above his belt.

He shuddered and lifted his head. She stared up at him with dazed, misty eyes and a swollen mouth.

"Shouldn't I touch you like that?" she whispered.

"I like letting you touch me like that," he replied huskily. "Unfasten it."

She flushed. "No, I couldn't!"

He held her hands against him, tenderly. "It's my body, isn't it?" he whispered. "If I don't mind, why should you? Aren't you curious?"

She was. She'd never wanted to touch a man that way, not even Ben when she was eighteen, and the realization shook her to her very shoes.

"Mandy," he said quietly, "I wouldn't seduce you. You'd have to want it, too, before I'd go that far."

"But..."

"But what, honey?" He bent and brushed his lips across her eyebrows, her closed eyes.

"Why...are you making love to me?"

His mouth smiled. "Because it feels good. Because I've never made love to a virgin."

She drew back and studied him curiously. "Never?" she whispered.

He shook his head, smiling. "You're my first."

She felt young and shy and a little embarrassed. Her eyes fell to his bare chest and she tingled just looking at it. "You're...my first," she confessed. "I never let any-one..."

"Never let anyone what, baby?" he whispered.

"Touch me...the way you did yesterday," she said finally.

"Here?" he asked softly, and brushed his knuckles over her soft breast.

"Y...yes," she faltered. She pressed close to him, shivering a little. He made her feel the wildest hungers.

His hands smoothed down her back and around to her hips. He moved her body lazily against his and caught his breath at the rush of sensation.

"Don't faint," he teased when she stiffened. "Think of it as private tutoring, Mandy. You're teaching me to be a gentleman. Let me teach you how to be a woman."

"I'm afraid!"

"I won't force you, precious," he whispered. "I won't ever force you. Let me show you what magic two people can make. Let me show you how sweet it can be."

He lifted her gently in his arms and looked down into her hungry gray eyes while his own blazed with pale blue flames. "I've got to have more of you than this," he whispered. "I want to feel you under me, just once, just for a few seconds."

"Carson...!" she moaned against his suddenly devouring mouth.

"Sweet," he whispered unsteadily, biting at her open, pleading lips. "God, you're so sweet...."

She felt him moving, but his mouth was seducing hers, and she clung to him and closed her eyes. She knew he was taking her to the bedroom. She knew, too, that once he had her down on the mattress and could feel her body yielding under the hard pressure of his own that no power on earth was going to stop him from taking her. Despite all the promises, he was on fire for her. And she was on fire for him. It was going to happen, and she wasn't even sorry. She sensed something in him that calmed her, that made her relax and return his tender caresses.

He carried her into the dark bedroom and laid her down on the soft coverlet. His hand traveled down from her shoulder, tracing her breasts, her waist, her stomach, the long line of her legs.

"I won't make you pregnant," he promised tautly, "and I won't hurt you. Okay?"

She trembled a little as she realized what he was saying, how explosive the passion between them had become. She felt his hands easing her dress down to her waist, over her hips. There was nothing under it but her briefs, and very gently he removed those, too, so that she was nude.

"You're trembling," he whispered as one big, warm hand rested on her belly. "You've never been nude with a man, either, have you?"

"No," she managed weakly.

"Your body feels like cream, Mandelyn," he said softly. He ran his hands over her, letting her feel their rough tenderness as he learned the soft contours of her body. "Slender, and beautiful, and soft to touch. Honey and spice and cotton candy..."

He bent and his mouth touched her stomach. She cried out, shocked by the intimacy of his lips there and by her own violent reaction to it.

"Hush, baby," he whispered in the darkness. "Hush now, there's nothing to be afraid of. I know what I'm doing."

"Yes, I know," she laughed shakily, "that's why I'm frightened. You...you said you wouldn't..."

"I want you," he whispered. "I've wanted you for so long, Mandy. I look at you and ache. Couldn't you pity me enough to give me one night?"

She wanted that night, too, but pity wasn't what was motivating her. She saw his head bend, his face a pale blur in the darkness and a piercing sweetness washed over her. Carson. He was Carson, and as familiar as her own face in the mirror, and no part of him was repulsive to her. She wanted him, too.

"Yes," she breathed. "Oh yes."

He seemed to freeze for a moment, and then he crushed her to him. "Let me turn on the light," he whispered hoarsely. "Let me watch you when it happens."

His hand went out before she could respond. He turned on the bedside lamp, flooding the room with light. She shrunk from him slightly in embarrassment. But he wasn't looking at her. His eyes were on the large color photograph in the ornate silver frame on the bedside table. His face paled. He reached out a hand and picked it up and stared down at the boyish face through the glass and his hand shook.

"Who?" he asked, his voice sounding dazed.

Her eyes barely focused. "It's Ben. Ben Hammack. He...was my fiancé."

Chapter Six

"Your fiancé?" He spoke as if he wasn't sure he'd heard her in the first place, and his eyes were riveted to the photograph.

The lovely, sultry sweetness between them had been dissipated by the stark light, and she fumbled with the coverlet, drawing it quickly over her body.

"You were engaged?" he persisted. "When?"

"Before I came out here," she faltered.

He stood up, replacing the photograph. His hand ran roughly through his disheveled hair, and she stared up at him helplessly. His shirt was still open and his mouth was faintly swollen from the pressure of the kisses they'd given each other. His eyes still bore traces of frustrated passion when they burned down into hers.

"Why didn't you tell me about him before?" he demanded. "When I asked if you'd ever wanted a man before. . . ."

She shivered at the accusation in his tone.

"It was when I was eighteen, Carson," she said, tugging the coverlet closer.

"Stop that," he growled. "I know every inch of you now, so stop behaving like a little prude. Was that a lie, too, are you really a virgin?"

"I haven't lied to you!"

"By omission!" he returned. "You never said anything about a fiancé! So where is he now? Did he throw you over? Are you still hung up on him, is that it?"

"Will you calm down?"

"Calm down, hell!" he ground out, glaring at her as he fumbled to light a cigarette. "I hurt all over. How could you let me make love to you with the image of another man sitting right here beside the bed...!''

She dropped her eyes, clutching the coverlet, embarrassed. "I was out of my head," she said miserably.

"So was I. I've never in my life wanted a woman so much. And if I hadn't turned on that damned light, we wouldn't be talking now. I'd be loving you."

The way he said it caused shimmers of sensation all over her bare body. "Yes, I know," she whispered.

"You'd have hated me for it," he added curtly.

"Would I?" she murmured.

His face hardened and he turned away from her to smoke the cigarette. "Where is he, this ex-fiancé?"

She sighed and stared down at her hands, unconsciously letting the coverlet slide a little. "He's dead."

That seemed to startle him. He turned around and came back to her, sitting down on the bed beside her. "Dead?"

She drew in a slow breath. "He was killed in a plane crash, on his way to a banker's convention in Washington, D.C. It was a small plane and it crashed into a hillside. You see, they...picked him up in pieces...."

He caught her hand reluctantly, and held it firmly in his. "I'm sorry. That would have made it worse."

She nodded. Her hand clung to his. "He was twenty-three, and I loved him with all my heart." Her eyes went past him to the photograph, and Ben looked very young to her now, with his blond hair tousled and his green eyes wicked and mischievous. "He came from a very old Charleston family. We had the same background and our families were friendly. He was brilliant, cultured and he could have gone to the moon. I could hardly believe it when he asked me to marry him. I wasn't his usual kind of girl at all. I was shy and quiet and he was so outgoing...." She shrugged and the coverlet, unnoticed, slipped again. Carson's eyes dropped as she spoke, his face going rigid as he stared at the soft, exposed curves. "After he died, I very nearly went crazy. Uncle had inherited the real estate office here and the ranch, and he'd planned to resell it. But when he saw what was happening to me, he moved us out here instead. I think it probably saved my sanity. I couldn't stop thinking about the way Ben died. It was killing me.''

He forced his eyes back up to hers. ''That's why you didn't date,'' he said suddenly.

''Of course.'' She stared at the photograph. ''I loved him so much. I was afraid to try again, to risk losing anybody else. I went out with one or two clients over the years, in a strictly platonic way. But most men won't be satisfied with just companionship, and when I realized that, I just gave up on it completely.''

''Now it makes sense,'' he murmured.

She looked up. ''What does?''

''The way you've been with me,'' he said quietly. ''As if you were starving to death for a little love.''

Her mouth trembled. ''I'm not!''

"Aren't you?" He reached out, and slowly peeled the coverlet back, letting it drop to her waist. And he looked down at her creamy, hard-tipped breasts with an expression that pleased her almost beyond bearing. "You see?" he said. "You like it when I look at you."

She did. Her hands trembled as she jerked the coverlet back in place, her face red, her eyes wild. "I don't!"

"Deny it until hell freezes over, but you would have given in before I turned on the light," he said hotly. "You wanted me, damn you!"

Her eyes closed and her hands trembled, clutching the fabric. She couldn't answer him, because he was right and they both knew it.

He got up abruptly and turned away. "God, this is rich," he said, a note of despair in his voice. He paced, smoking like a furnace. "I thought it was because you were a virgin, that being made love to was new and you were learning things about me that you liked. And all the time, I was substituting for a ghost."

That shocked her. "No," she began, because she couldn't let him believe that. It just wasn't true.

"A dead man. A shrine." He seemed to get angrier as he went along. His eyes burned when he whirled suddenly to glare down at her. "Why did you let me bring you in here?" he burst out.

She shivered a little at his tone. "I don't know."

He lifted the cigarette to his lips jerkily and his eyes went involuntarily to the photograph. "You were still mourning him when we met, weren't you?" he asked. "That's why you got so mad at me when I made a pass."

"I couldn't bear the thought of another relationship," she hedged, staring down at the coverlet.

"Hell! You mean, you couldn't bear the thought of some ruffian wanting you. I didn't measure up, did I? I wasn't fit to wear his shoes!"

"Carson, no!" she said fiercely. "No, it isn't like that!"

"I'm rough and hard and I've got no manners," he ground out. "I don't come from a socially prominent family and I didn't go to Harvard. So I'm not even in the running. I never was. You've built him into a little tin god and you keep his picture by your bed to remind you that you've climbed into the grave with him, isn't that it!"

She got up, dragging the cover with her, and went to stand in front of him, her eyes wide, her heart aching. He was hurting, and she'd done that to him. All because of a past she couldn't let go of.

"Carson," she said softly, reaching out to touch his hard arm.

The muscles contracted. "Don't do it, honey," he cautioned in a dangerously soft voice. "I'm feeling pretty raw right now."

"Well, so am I," she burst out. "I didn't want you to start pushing your way into my life, to back me into a corner! I didn't start kissing *you*...!"

"As if you ever would have," he said quietly. His eyes were bleak, his face pale and hard. "I guess I've been dreaming. You're as far out of my league as I am out of yours. It's just as well that you aren't civilizing me for yourself, isn't it?"

Her smooth shoulders lifted and fell. "I guess so." She stared down at his boots.

"We'd better forget the dancing lessons," he said coldly. "And before you start getting the wrong idea about what happened tonight, I told you once that I've been without a woman for a while. You went to my head, that's all."

That hurt. She had to fight down a flood of tears. Her eyes lifted proudly to his. "Same here," she said curtly.

"Yes, I know that," he said with a mocking smile. He nodded toward the photograph. "Why don't you take that to bed with you, and see if it makes you burn the way I did."

She lifted her hand, but he caught her wrist and held it easily, letting her feel his strength.

It brought her to her senses like a cold shower of rain. "You can let go," she said defeatedly. "I won't try to hit you."

He dropped her wrist as if it had scorched him. "Hadn't you better put your clothes on? You might catch cold—if ice can."

Her eyes flashed at him. "I wasn't cold with you," she said fiercely.

The hasty words seemed to kindle something in him. His eyes narrowed and glittered. He reached out and caught the back of her head and before she could turn her mouth, his lips crushed down on it. He twisted her mouth under his, hurting her for an instant, before he lifted it again and glared into her eyes.

"Firecracker," he said heavily, "if you weren't worshipping a damned ghost, I'd throw you down on that bed and make you beg for my body. But as things stand, I'd say we both had a lucky escape."

He let her go and strode out of the room. Seconds later, the door slammed, and she heard his car start and roar away. The house was so still that she could hear the clock in

the living room, like a bomb. Tick. Tick.
Tick.

She hardly slept at all that night. Her eyes
had been well and truly opened by Carson's
cutting remarks. She hadn't realized just
how much she'd been living in the past until
he'd accused her of making a shrine for Ben.
Of trying to climb into the grave with him.

With a cup of coffee in her hand the next
morning, she sat on the edge of her bed and
stared at the photograph. Ben looked im-
possibly young. And as she gazed at his picture, she remembered how things had been
all those years ago. It hadn't been a great
love affair. He'd been a handsome, eligible
bachelor with a magnetic personality, and
she'd been young and shy and flattered by
his attention. But over the years, she had
built his image into something unrealistic. It
had taken Carson's feverish lovemaking to
teach her that.

She flushed remembering how it had been
between them the night before. He'd been so
tender, so achingly tender and patient. And
if he hadn't seen that photograph...

She got to her feet, frowning, and paced the floor. Her eyes went involuntarily to the bed and her mind traced, torturously, every wild second she'd spent on it the night before. Carson, kissing her with such sweet hunger, Carson touching her in ways no one else ever had. Carson, looking at her with eyes that ate her. Loving her.

Her eyes closed. It had been loving, of a kind. He'd wanted her quite desperately, and not for the first time last night. He'd wanted her for a long time; perhaps from the very beginning. But he hadn't let her know it. Not until he asked her for those "lessons." And now she had to wonder if that had been only a means to an end. If he'd decided it was past time to do something about his violent hunger.

Did he care, though? That was the thing that tortured her. Was it just a physical hunger that he was trying to satisfy, or did he feel something for her? And did it matter to her?

She put her cup back in the kitchen and got dressed to go to work. It probably was a moot point now, she thought miserably. If the way he'd looked and talked last night was any indication, he'd never want to see her again.

Angie had several messages from prospective clients which Mandelyn took to her office and stared at blankly. It was an hour before she could get into the mood to work, and even then she did it halfheartedly. She spent the day staring at the phone, hoping that Carson would call. But by five o'clock, he hadn't, and she realized that he probably wouldn't want to. She went home in a daze and spent the evening staring at the walls.

Friday came dragging around, finally, and Patty stuck her head in the door of the real estate office to remind Mandelyn about coming to her party that night.

"The party?" Mandelyn felt sick all over. Carson had been going to take her. "I...I don't know, Patty."

"You've got to come," she prodded. "Carson said he was bringing you."

Mandelyn's heart jumped. "Recently?" she asked hesitantly.

"This morning, when I went out to give his bull the all-clear." Patty grinned. "He was in a foul mood until I mentioned that the Gibson boys were coming to play for me. He used to sit in with them years ago. He's a heck of a good guitarist, you know."

"No, I didn't," Mandelyn said slowly. There were a lot of things she didn't know about Carson, it seemed.

"Anyway, they'll probably jam for a while. It's going to be lots of fun. See you about six!"

"Okay," she replied with a wan smile.

"I wish I could come," Angie sighed when Patty was gone. "I've got to babysit my sister's kids. Three of them. All pre-schoolers. Patty was going to introduce me to a guy who'll be there. Now I'll have to load a gun and look for my own. All on account of my sister's bridge game."

Mandelyn almost laughed at the younger woman's miserable look. "I'd offer to stand in for you, if I could," she said, and really would have considered it. She wasn't looking forward to spending an evening around Carson, whom she was certain hated her.

"I'd almost let you," Angie replied. "But don't worry, I'll survive. I was a girl scout."

"I guess that would help."

"Survival training usually does, with preschoolers," Angie murmured, and reached for the phone, which was ringing off the hook. She pressed the "hold" button. "It's for you. Mr. Wayne."

Mandelyn's heart tried to reach into her throat. She was tempted to have Angie tell him she couldn't come to the phone. Amazing, how he brought out these cowardly instincts of hers.

"Okay," she said, and wandered slowly back into her office. She picked up the phone with trembling hands. "Hello," she said professionally.

"Can you be ready by five-thirty?" Carson asked coldly, and without any preliminaries.

The sound of his voice made her ache. She closed her eyes and wrapped the cord around her fingers. "Yes," she said.

"Patty's idea," he reminded her. "I'd as soon have gone alone."

"Well, if you'd rather...!" she began, feeling hurt and hating him.

"Hell, yes, I would, but I won't give this whole town something to gossip about by refusing to go with you. And neither will you. Be ready." And he slammed the phone down.

Mandelyn slammed her own receiver down, gave a furious groan and heaved a telephone directory at the door.

Angie, shocked, rushed to the doorway. "Are you okay?" she asked, her eyes wide and fascinated. She'd never seen the very proper Miss Bush throw things.

"No," Mandelyn said with blazing eyes. "No, I'm not. I'll kill him one day. I'll shoot him through the heart. I'll feed him cactus branches. I'll..."

"Mr. Wayne?" Angie gasped. "But you're friends."

"Me? Friends with that animal?"

Angie stood quietly, fishing for the right words.

"I'm going home," Mandelyn said. She grabbed up her purse and stormed out the door. "Close up, will you?"

"Sure. But..."

"I'll put alum in his punch," Mandelyn was muttering. "I'll put burrs under his saddle...."

Angie just shook her head. "It must be love," she murmured drily, and then laughed at the thought. Miss Bush and Carson Wayne would be the mismatch of the century. Miss Bush was cool and proper and Carson was a wild man. She couldn't picture the two of them in love. Not in a million years. She went back to her desk and started clearing it.

Mandelyn sped home at such a rate that she attracted the attention of Sheriff's deputy Danny Burton. Considering that Danny hardly ever noticed speeders, that was quite a feat.

She pulled over when she heard the siren, and sat there fuming until the short, dark-headed deputy came around to her window.

"Let's see your license, Miss Bush, and your registration," Danny said drily. "Might as well do the thing properly. Where's the fire—that's the other part of my speech."

"The fire is going to be under Carson Wayne, just as soon as I can find some wood and matches," she said venomously.

He stared at her. "You're his pal," he reminded her.

"That rattlesnake?" she burst out.

He cleared his throat and took the license and registration from her shaking hands. "He must have done something pretty bad to rile you. Poor old feller."

"Poor old feller? He locked you in a closet, have you forgotten already?"

He grinned. "He's been locking me in closets for six years. I've got used to it. Besides, when he sobers up, he always buys me lunch at Rosie's. He ain't a bad guy." He handed back the license and finished writing up the ticket. "Why were you in such a rush?" he asked.

"Patty's party's tonight," she murmured.

"Oh, yeah. I'm going, too. Looks like it's going to be a real hummer, especially since the Gibsons and Carson will be together again. Damn, that Carson can make a guitar sing!''

Why did everybody know that except her? It made her even madder. She took the ticket with a sigh.

"Now slow down," he cautioned. "If you wreck the car, you can't very well go dancing tonight, can you, Miss Bush?''

She sighed. "I guess not. Sorry, Danny. I'll slow down.''

"Good girl. See you later.''

"Yes. See you later.''

She drove home under a black cloud. Even after she'd dressed in a full red printed skirt and a white peasant blouse, with low-heeled shoes, she still hadn't cooled down. She felt wild. Furious at Carson, furious at the circumstances that forced her to be near him. She only wanted to close him out of her life and forget that he even existed. He was haunting her!

When he drove up, her heart began to race wildly. She didn't want to see him, she didn't want him near her! Her body tingled as she opened the door and looked at him. He was wearing jeans and a red print Western shirt with a red bandana. His brown boots were the new ones they'd bought together in Phoenix. They were highly polished, and matched the tan hat he'd bought to go with them. And he looked so handsome and virile that she ached.

His own eyes were busy, sweeping over her body in the unfamiliar casual clothing. Her hair was loose around her shoulders, and she seemed smaller and much more feminine than before. His teeth ground together and his face grew harder.

"Ready?" he asked curtly.

"When I get my purse and shawl, yes," she returned icily. She jerked them up from the sofa and locked the door behind her.

He opened the door of the Thunderbird for her, but she hardly noticed. She was still angry at his curtness.

He got in and started the car, then sped out onto the highway.

"Keep that up and you'll get one, too," she said, staring straight ahead.

"Get one, what?" he asked.

"Speeding ticket."

His eyebrows jerked up. "The way you drive, you got a ticket? Sheriff Wilson hire a new man or something?"

She continued to stare out the window. "Danny gave it to me."

"Pull the other one. Danny never stops anybody."

"I was doing ninety-five at the time.'

The car went all over the road before he righted it. "Ninety-five, on these roads?"

"Go ahead, make some nasty remark," she challenged, her eyes glittering up at him. "Go on, I dare you!"

His eyes studied hers for an instant before they went back to the road. "In a temper?"

"You ought to know. Yours isn't so sweet today, either."

"I think I'm entitled to a bad temper, considering how I got it."

She flushed and wouldn't look at him. She wouldn't talk to him, either. He didn't seem to mind. He drove all the way to Patty's house without saying a word.

Chapter Seven

"Carson! Mandy! It's about time you got here!" Patty laughed, rushing forward to grab Carson by the arm. She looked nervous and flustered, and nearby, Jake was talking to a group of cowboys.

Mandelyn had never in her life felt such a violent urge to hit another woman. Patty, blissfully unaware of her friend's reaction, clung closer to Carson's sleeve and grinned.

"The Gibsons have been waiting for you," she teased. "Jack said he wouldn't even play if you didn't come."

Carson laughed, and Mandelyn could have cried, because it seemed that the day was long gone when he would laugh with her that way.

"In that case, I'd better get over there, I reckon. You look sweet," he added in a soft drawl, glancing down at Patty's blue polka-dotted dress and white shoes.

"Thank you," Patty said, and curtsied. Her eyes flirted with him. "It's nice to have my efforts appreciated."

Her hair was loose tonight, too, and she'd never looked less tomboyish. Jake glanced at her out of the corner of one eye and scowled. Mandelyn was the only one who caught that look, and she wondered for an instant if Jake might be jealous. What an odd idea. Carson's foreman never looked at women.

"Excuse us, Mandy," Patty said politely and dragged Carson away. He went like a lamb, without a backward glance.

Mandelyn felt out of place. She was in no humor to enjoy partying this evening. But Jake seemed to sense that, and excused himself from the other cowboys to join her.

"You look as out of place as I feel, Miss Bush," he said wryly. "I'm not much of a partygoer."

"And I'm not in much of a party mood," she sighed, clasping her hands tightly in front of her. She was watching Carson. He shook hands with the four brothers at the bandstand and accepted a big guitar from one of them. Tossing his hat to Patty, he sat down with them.

"Quite a treat, to hear the boss play," Jake murmured. "He doesn't do that very often these days."

"I've never heard him play," she mentioned.

He glanced down at her. "I'm not much surprised. He probably thinks you'd prefer something classical."

"Everybody seems to know me better than I know myself," she sighed. Actually, she liked Country-Western music very much.

They were tuning up and Carson said something and they all laughed. He seemed so different here, with people he knew. He was relaxed and cheerful and outgoing . . . a stranger. He seemed to sense her watching him and glanced up, but his eyes weren't smiling. She dropped her own to avoid the accusation and frank dislike in his gaze.

"You two have a falling out?" Jake asked quietly. "He's been pure hell the past few days."

"I noticed," she said shortly.

Jake shrugged and leaned back against the doorway to listen. The Gibson brother who led the band gave them the beat and they swung into a fast, furious rendition of "San Antonio Rose." The others muted their own instruments, two guitars, a bass and a fiddle, and Carson's lean fingers flew across the steel strings of his guitar with beautiful precision. Mandelyn gaped at him. She'd expected that he'd be passable, but what he was doing with the instrument made her knees weak. He was expert.

"Good, ain't he?" Jake grinned. "I used to fuss because he wouldn't go professional, but he said running all over the country with a band wasn't his idea of fun. He liked cattle better."

She watched Carson with sad, quiet eyes. "He's marvelous," she said softly, and her tone hinted that she didn't mean only as a musician.

Jake glanced at her curiously, puzzled by her rapt expression, by the odd look in her gray eyes. So that was it. He looked back at his boss and smiled slowly.

Patty was standing near him, clapping and laughing. He glanced up at her and grinned as he finished the piece. The band gave the last chord and cheered.

"How about 'Choices'?" Jake yelled.

Carson looked up and frowned when he saw Jake standing beside Mandelyn.

"Yes, how about it?" Patty seconded. "Come on, Carson, do it!"

"He wrote that one," Jake told Mandelyn. "We made him copyright it, but he never would let anyone record it."

She studied the man in the red checkered shirt and couldn't fathom him. He gave in to the prodding finally. What he did to the guitar then was so sweet and heady that Mandelyn felt a rush of emotion. It was a love song, pure and simple. All about two different worlds with no bridge between them. And he sang it in a deep, sultry voice that would have made a dedicated spinster's heart whirl. He had the sexiest voice Mandelyn had ever heard, and she watched, spellbound, while he sang. His eyes lifted once, glanced off hers, and went to Patty. He smiled. And Mandelyn closed her eyes on a wave of pain.

When he finished, there was a moment's pause, and then uproarious applause.

"And he's raising cattle, can you believe it?" Patty burst out. She laughed and bent over to kiss Carson firmly on the mouth. "You're great!"

Mandelyn felt sick. Jake said something rough under his breath. He looked down, noticed her sudden paleness and took her arm.

"Are you okay, ma'am?" he asked gently.

"Just a little wobbly," she laughed nervously. "I've been working hard lately."

"You're not alone. So has boss man."

The band had started to play some dance music now. Jake glanced at his boss, who was glaring in his direction. He glared back.

"Would you dance with me, Miss Bush?" he asked.

"Well . . ."

"He dared me," he said curtly, glancing past her to Carson. "Two can play that game."

"I don't understand."

He led her onto the dance floor. "Never mind," he grumbled. He shuffled around, much the way Carson had the night she'd taught him to dance.

Patty was looking at the two of them curiously. Jake gave her a cold smile and whirled Mandelyn around.

Mandelyn looked up, and saw murderous fury in his face. So that was it, she realized, Jake and Carson were competing for Patty!

Her eyes fell to Jake's collar. She sighed miserably. It seemed that she wasn't the only one suffering. So Jake wanted Patty, too. He wouldn't win. She knew instinctively that Carson would beat the younger man in any kind of competition, especially when it came to loving.

"Are you sure you feel okay?" Jake asked quietly.

"Not really," she admitted. "But I'll make it."

He smiled at her. "Yes, ma'am, I imagine you will."

The evening wore on, and Carson never left the brothers Gibson for a minute. He played and Patty stayed by him. Mandelyn sat down after the first dance, leaving Jake to circulate among the other women. There was a large crowd, larger, she suspected, than Patty had anticipated. But everyone seemed to be having a great time.

Patty brought Carson a beer and held it to his firm lips while he played. Mandelyn got more and more morose, until finally she was praying that it would all be over and she could go home. She'd never been more miserable in her life. Watching Patty and Carson ogle each other was more than she could bear.

Eventually, Jake joined her again, squatting down beside her chair to watch with narrowed angry eyes as Carson and Patty talked while the band was preparing to play their closing song.

"Patty looks nice," she said quietly.

He shrugged. His eyes went to a piece of string that he was twisting into a hangman's noose in his hands. "Yeah, I guess so."

She felt a sudden kinship with Jake and impulsively murmured, "You, too, huh?"

He looked up, flushed, and looked down again. "Maybe it's contagious."

"Maybe it's curable."

He laughed reluctantly. "Reckon? If you find an antidote, share it with me."

"Same here."

He glared toward Carson and Patty. "It's disgusting. She's too young for him."

Her eyes widened as she gaped at him. "You're almost Carson's age. She's a little young for you, too, isn't she?"

"What's that got to do with anything?" he grumbled.

She only smiled. He probably felt as miserable as she did. She laid a gentle hand on his broad shoulder. "Don't let it get you down. Take up the guitar and practice."

"I can't even carry a tune," he sighed. He looked up. "You might study veterinary medicine."

"I faint at the sight of blood," she confessed.

He smiled warmly. "I guess we're both out of the running."

"I guess." She smiled back.

It was too bad they didn't look across the room at that moment. If they had, they'd have seen two furious pairs of eyes glaring at them from the bandstand.

Carson hadn't danced one single dance all evening. But as the band launched into the "Tennessee Waltz" he led Patty to the floor and held her close during that last dreamy tune.

He shook hands with the Gibson boys, bent down to brush his lips over Patty's cheek and thanked her for the evening. And then he turned to Mandelyn with such evident reluctance that she wanted to scream and throw things.

"Thanks, Patty," she said with forced politeness. "I had a lovely time."

"Good. I'm glad," Patty said with equally forced politeness. "See you."

Mandelyn shot out the door past Carson and climbed into the Thunderbird with ill-concealed impatience. He sauntered along, taking his time, cocking his hat at a jaunty angle.

"You're in a flaming rush," he remarked as he climbed in beside her and started the car.

"I'm tired," she said. Her gaze went out the window to the ghostly shapes of the saguaro cactus against the sky.

"From what?" he asked. "You only danced once. With Jake."

"Jake dances very well."

"He stepped all over you."

She stared ahead as the headlights penetrated the darkness. She almost said, "So did you the other night." But she wasn't going to fall into that trap. She kept her silence.

"Patty looked good, didn't she?" he remarked. "I haven't seen her let her hair down and wear a dress in years."

"She looked lovely," she said through her teeth.

He glanced at her and away again. "Want to declare a truce? At least until the ballet? It would be a shame to waste those tickets."

"I'm not going to any damned ballet with you," she said vehemently. "And, no, I don't want to declare a truce. I hate you!"

He whistled through his teeth. "Temper, temper."

"I've seen so much of yours lately that it's affected my mind," she said sweetly.

"I thought it was your loving memory of your late fiancé that had done that," he said.

She turned, eyes glittering. "Stop this car and let me out, right now!" she demanded.

Amazingly, he did just that. He stopped the car abruptly. "Okay! If you want to walk, go ahead. It's seven more miles."

"Fine. I love long walks!" She got out, slammed the door violently, and started down the road. He took off, leaving skid marks behind him.

She couldn't believe he'd really done that. She stood gaping at his disappearing taillights and tears welled up in her soft gray eyes. She felt lost and frightened, and she really did hate him then. Leaving her alone in the darkness on a deserted highway.

She looked around nervously. She could hardly see her feet at all, and she just knew there were rattlesnakes all around her. Diamondbacks! She began to move gingerly, wishing she had a flashlight, wishing she could have kept her stupid mouth shut. She'd set him off again, just when his temper seemed to be improving.

Her lips trembled. She was really afraid now, and there wasn't a soul in sight. There were no houses, no cars, no nothing. She rounded a curve, shaking, and there was the Thunderbird. Carson was leaning against it, smoking a cigarette.

"Damn you!" she bit off, but she was crying and the words hardly registered.

He said something rough and threw the cigarette to the ground. The next minute, she was in his arms.

He held her much too close, rocking her, his arms warm and hard and protective. And she cried, because of the miserable night she'd had, because of the way things were between them.

"I'm sorry," he said at her ear. "I'm sorry."

She trembled at the deep softness in his voice. "I was afraid," she admitted unsteadily.

His arms tightened slowly. She felt the length of him and something kindled in her own body. Her eyes closed. She clung to him, her hands flat against the rippling muscles of his back, her breasts crushing softly into his chest, her legs brushing the powerful muscles of his. Out on the desert, a coyote howled and the wind blew. And Mandelyn had never felt so safe, or so happy.

"We'd better get home," he said after a minute. "Come on."

He held her hand, led her to the car, and put her in on the driver's side. She slid reluctantly across, wondering what would have happened if she'd stayed close to him. Probably, she thought miserably, he'd have pushed her away.

Driving, it was only a short way from there to her house. He stopped outside the door, but he didn't switch off the engine.

"I . . . would you like some coffee?" she offered.

"No, thanks. I've got to get some sleep. We're moving cattle in the morning."

"Oh. Thanks for the ride."

"Sure. Any time."

She opened her door and hesitated. "About the ballet . . ."

"Since I've already got the tickets, it would be a shame to waste them. I can't take anyone but you with me." He laughed shortly. "Patty would laugh her head off."

Her teeth ground together. "No doubt. What night?"

"Wednesday. We'll need to leave here by five, to get there in time."

"I'll close up early." She got out, hating him more than ever, and slammed the door.

"Mandelyn."

She paused. He'd rolled down the passenger window and was leaning across. "Yes?"

"This will be the last time," he said curtly. "I think when we get through with the ballet, I'll have learned enough to cope."

"Good. It was getting a bit boring, wasn't it?" she asked coldly.

"I'll tell you something, honey," he said quietly. "I've about decided that I like my world better than I like yours. Mine has the advantage of real people and honest emotions. Yours is an old house with elegant furniture and the warmth of a tomb. Speaking of which, there's yours. Why don't you go and moon over your lost love?"

Her fists clenched by her sides. "If I had a gun, I'd blow you in half," she spat.

"Hell. If you had a gun, you'd shoot yourself in the foot. Good night."

He rolled up the window while she was stomping onto the porch. She jammed the key into the lock and broke it in half as he roared away.

Her eyes widened. The back door had an old lock and she didn't have its key. The windows were down and locked. Now what was she going to do?

With a heavy sigh, she went out and got a big rock. She took it to the side of the house and flung it through the window. The sound of shattering glass made her feel a little better, even though she knew she was going to have an interesting story to tell the repairman in the morning.

Unfortunately, the handyman she had to call was out working on the renovations at Carson's place. He was too busy to come. She managed to talk his wife into giving her the number of a man who put in windows in his spare time. She contacted him and got a promise that he'd do the window first thing Monday morning. Meanwhile she got a locksmith to come out and fix the door. She hadn't asked the handyman's wife how things were going over at Carson's, although she was curious about how the house would look when they got through. Carson's preparations were none of her business. Probably Patty knew, though, she thought miserably.

She went up to Phoenix and spent the rest of the weekend there just to get away. How drastically things had changed in just a few short weeks, she thought. She and Carson had been on the verge of friendship, but those few days together had changed everything. Actually, she decided, that long, hard kiss he'd given her behind the bar had done it. She'd been curious about him after that, and when he'd made a pass, she hadn't had the strength to put him off. She'd wanted to know how he would be as a lover. And now she knew, and the knowledge was eating her up like acid. She'd never known that a man could be so tender, so protective and possessive. She could have had all that, if not for Carson's obsession with changing to suit Patty.

Patty. She went out to the balcony of her hotel room and glared over the city's lights. The wind tore through her hair and she drank in the sounds and smells of the night. He'd kissed Patty at her party. Why had he done that? She closed her eyes and she could almost hear Carson's deep, slow voice as he sang. She leaned her head against the wall and wondered how it would be to sit with him on his porch late on a summer evening while he sang to her. And if there were children, they could sit on her lap. . . .

The thought was intensely painful. She remembered how it had been that night, the night she'd wanted him so much. If only he hadn't turned on the light and seen Ben's photograph.

Dear Ben. Her bastion against emotional involvement. Her wall that kept love out of her life. And now she was twenty-six and alone and she'd lost the only man in the world she wanted to live with.

Of course, she hadn't a chance against Patty. She'd always known that. Carson was too fond of the woman. She turned back into her room. How odd that he wanted to learn cultural things for Patty, though. Especially when Patty seemed to like country things and country people. How very odd.

She went back to Sweetwater late Sunday night, feeling drained and no more refreshed than before. It was going to be another long week.

It didn't help that Patty came into her office early Monday morning with a complaint about the property.

"The roof leaks," she grumbled. "It poured rain here, and you told me that roof was sound. I had ten half-drowned cats before I thought to check."

"I'm sorry," Mandelyn said formally. "The previous owner assured me he'd had a new roof put on recently. You know I'd never purposely misrepresent a property," she added. "You're going to have trouble finding a roofer. Carson seems to have every workman in town out at his place."

"It's coming along nicely, too," Patty remarked. "He's had new furniture put in the house and carpeting . . . it's a showplace already. Once they get the new roof on, and the painting finished, it will make most houses in the valley look like outbuildings.''

''You'll like that, I'm sure,'' Mandelyn murmured under her breath.

''I'll call Carson and see if he can loan me his roofer,'' Patty said suddenly. ''Why didn't I think of that myself?''

''Good idea,'' Mandelyn said with a wan smile.

Patty started out the door and paused. ''Uh, Jake spent a lot of time with you at the party,'' she murmured. ''Seen him since?''

''I've been out of town,'' Mandelyn said noncommittally. ''I haven't seen anybody.''

''Jake's been out of town, too,'' Patty said, her smile disappearing. She opened the door and went out, slamming it behind her.

Angie glanced up from her typewriter with a curious stare. ''You and Jake . . . ?''

''Oh, shut up,'' Mandelyn said. ''I haven't been anywhere with Jake. She's just mad because Carson isn't running after her fast enough, I suppose. He isn't good enough for her. . . .''

She went into her office and slammed the door, too. Angie shrugged and went back to work.

Mandelyn didn't hear from Carson at all. Wednesday, she went ahead and dressed to go to the ballet, feeling not at all happy about it. She'd rather have stayed home and bawled. It was how she felt. She wasn't even sure that Carson would show up at all. He was getting to be wildly unpredictable.

She chose a floor-length blue velvet gown with white accessories and put her hair up with a blue velvet ribbon. She kept remembering that blue velvet ribbon in Carson's car, and wished she could get it out of her mind. He must not have gotten it from her, after all.

At five-thirty, he still hadn't shown up, and she was on her way back to her bedroom to change her clothes when she heard a car pull up.

She felt as nervous as a girl on her first date. She was probably overdressed, but she'd wanted to look pretty for him. That was idiotic. But she couldn't help herself.

She opened the door, and found him in a tuxedo. That was one item they hadn't bought together, and she couldn't help but stare. He was so striking that she couldn't drag her eyes away. He had the perfect physique for a tuxedo, and the whiteness of the silk shirt he was wearing made his complexion darker, his hair blacker. His blue eyes were dark, too, as they looked down at her.

"You . . . look very nice," she faltered.

"So do you," he said, but his eyes were cold. Like his face. "We'd better go."

She followed him outside, forgetting her wrap in the excitement. They were halfway to Phoenix before she remembered.

"My stole," she exclaimed.

"You aren't likely to freeze to death," he said curtly.

"I didn't say I was, Carson," she replied.

He tugged at his tie. "I'll be glad when this is over," he grumbled.

"It was your idea," she said sweetly.

"I've had some pretty bad ideas lately."

"Yes, I know."

His eyes drifted slowly over her. "Was it necessary to wear a dress that was cut to the navel?" he asked harshly.

She wouldn't let him rattle her. "It was the only dressy thing I had."

"Left over from the days when you dated the eligible banker and were in the thick of Charleston society, no doubt," he said mockingly.

She closed her eyes and wouldn't answer him.

"No retort?" he chided.

"I won't argue with you, Carson," she said. "I'm through fighting. I've got no stomach for it anymore."

She felt that way, too, as if all the life had been drained out of her.

"You, through fighting?" he laughed coldly.

"People change."

"Not enough. They never change enough to suit other people. I'm dressed up in this damned monkey suit going to a form of entertainment I don't understand or even like. And it isn't going to change what I am. I'm no fancy dude. I never will be. I've accepted that."

"Will your fancy woman accept it?" she laughed unpleasantly. "Will she want you the way you are?"

"Maybe not," he replied. "But that's how she'll take me."

"So masterful!" she taunted. "How exciting for her!"

He turned his head slowly and the look in his eyes was hot and dangerous. "You'll push me too far one day."

She turned her gaze toward the city lights of Phoenix.

He pulled up near the auditorium and parked. There was a crowd, and she kept close to Carson, feeling a little nervous around all the strangers.

He glanced down at her, frowning. "Aren't you afraid to get that close to me?" he taunted.

"I'm less afraid of you than I am of them," she confessed. "I don't like crowds."

He stopped dead and looked down at her with narrow, searching eyes. "But you like culture, don't you, honey?"

The sarcasm in his voice was cutting. She looked back at him quietly. "I like men with deep voices singing love songs, too," she said.

He seemed disconcerted for a minute. He turned away, guiding her into the throng with a puzzled frown.

Everything seemed to go wrong. Their tickets were for another night, and Carson was told so, politely but firmly.

"Wrong night, hell," he told the small man at the door. Then he grinned and that meant trouble. "Listen, sonny, they were supposed to be for tonight. I'm here. And I'm staying.'

"Sir, please lower your voice," the little man pleaded, looking nervously around him.

"Lower it? I plan on raising it quite a bit," Carson returned. "You want trouble, you can have it. In spades."

Mandelyn closed her eyes. This was getting to be a pattern. Why did she let herself in for this kind of embarrassment?

"Please go in, sir. I'm sure the mixup is our fault," the small man said loudly and with a forced smile.

Carson nodded at him and smiled coldly. "I'm sure it is. Come on, Mandy."

He guided her into the auditorium and seated her on the aisle beside him. He stuck out his long legs and stared down at the program. He scowled.

"*Swan Lake?*" he asked, staring at the photos in the printed program. He glanced at Mandelyn. "You mean we came all this way to watch some woman dressed up like a damned bird parading across the stage?"

Oh, God, she prayed, give him laryngitis!

Around them were sharp, angry murmurs. Mandelyn touched his hand. "Carson, ballet is an art form. It's dancing. You know that."

"Dancing, okay. But parading around in a bird suit, and her a grown woman?"

She tapped him on the arm with her program.

"Swatting flies?" he asked.

She hid her face behind her program, slid down in the seat, and prayed for a power failure. There were too many lights. Everyone could see that the loud man was with her.

He continued to make loud comments until the lights went down. Mandelyn almost sagged with relief in the darkness. But she should have known better. The minute the orchestra began to play and the lead ballerina finally appeared, he sat up straight and leaned forward.

"When does the ballet start?" he demanded.

"It just did!" she hissed.

"All she's doing is running around the stage!" he protested.

"Shut up, could you!" the man behind Carson said curtly.

Carson turned around and glared through the darkness. "I paid for my ticket, just like you did. So shut up yourself. Or step outside."

The man was twice Carson's age, and rather chubby. He cleared his throat, trying to look belligerent. But he held his peace.

Carson glanced down at Mandelyn. "Something in your shoe?" he asked. "Why are you hiding?"

"I'm not hiding," she choked, red-faced as she sat back up.

He was staring at the stage. Out came a muscular male dancer, and Carson gaped and caught his breath and burst out laughing.

"Oh, do be quiet," she squeaked.

"Hell, look at that," he roared. "He looks like he's wearing long johns. And what the hell is that between his legs . . . ?"

"Oh, God," she moaned, burying her hands in her face.

"Better not bother Him, lady," the man behind her suggested. "If He hears what that man's saying, He'll strike him dead."

Mandelyn was only hoping for hoarseness, but it didn't happen. Carson kept laughing, and she couldn't stand it another minute. Everyone near them was talking; they had disrupted the entire performance.

She climbed over Carson and ran for the front door. She made her way through the lobby and into the women's rest room. She stayed there for a long time, crimson to the roots of her hair. How could he? He knew better than to behave like that. He'd done it deliberately, and she knew it. He'd been trying to embarrass her, to humiliate her in front of what he thought was her own set. And that hurt most of all. That he'd done it to wound her.

Carson was waiting for her, his head down, glaring at his dress shoes when she came back out of the rest room. He heard her step and looked up.

His eyes were dark blue. Quiet. Searching. He took his hands out of his pockets and moved toward her.

"You've had your fun," she said with dignity. "Or revenge. Or whatever you like to call it. Now that you've ruined my evening, please take me home.'

His jaw tightened. "Miss Bush of Charleston, to the back teeth," he said mockingly. "Dignity first."

"I have very little dignity left, thank you," she replied. "And I'm through trying to civilize you. I know a hopeless case when I see one."

His eyes flashed. "Giving up?"

"Oh, yes," she said with a cool smile. "And I wish your woman joy of you, Carson. Maybe if she can put a bridle on you, she can tell people you're a horse and don't know any better manners."

The expression that crossed his face was indescribable. He turned on his heel and led the way out the door. She followed him stiffly, standing aside to let him unlock her side of the car.

It was a long, harrowing ride home. He turned on the radio and let it play to fill the silence. When they pulled up in front of her house, she was too drained to even notice what was playing. He'd told her in actions just how much contempt he felt for her.

"Mandelyn," he said.

She didn't even look at him. "Goodbye, Carson."

"I'd like to talk to you," he said through his teeth. "Explain something."

"What could you possibly say that would be of interest to me? You and I have absolutely nothing in common," she said with cool hauteur and a look that spoke volumes. "Do invite me to the wedding. I'll see if I can find something homespun to wear. And I'll even send you a wedding gift. How would you like a set of matching knives for your table? After all, you have to have something to eat your peas with, don't you? Just the thing for a savage like you!"

She got out of the car, slammed the door and marched up the steps. It took her the rest of the night to try to forget the look on Carson's face when she'd said that to him. And she cried herself to sleep for her own cruelty. She hadn't meant it. She'd only wanted to hurt him as much as he'd hurt her. He'd as much as told her that her world was shoddy and superficial. It had been the killing blow. Because she understood all at once why it hurt so much. She was in love with Carson. And she'd just lost him forever.

Chapter Eight

Mandelyn couldn't even go to work the next day, she was so sick about what had happened the night before. She shouldn't have behaved so badly, even though Carson had provoked her. She shouldn't have hurt him like that.

"I've got a migraine," she told Angie. She knew she sounded unwell from crying all night. "If anyone needs me, tell them I'll be back tomorrow, okay?"

Angie hesitated. "Uh, Patty came by as soon as I opened up."

"Oh?"

"Yes. She asked if I knew that Carson was in jail."

Mandelyn gripped the receiver hard. "What?"

"She said he went on a bender last night and dared Jake to call you. Danny had to lock him up. They said he set new records for broken glass, and to top it all off, he ran his Thunderbird into Jim Handel's new swimming pool."

Her eyes closed and tears welled up behind her swollen eyelids. Because of her, she knew. Because of the way she'd hurt him.

"Is he still there?" she asked after a minute.

"No, ma'am. Patty bailed him out. She took him over to her place to look after him. He's pretty bruised and battered, but she says he'll be okay. She, uh, thought you might want to know."

"Well I don't," she said quietly. "I don't want to hear about Carson Wayne again as long as I live. See you tomorrow, Angie," she added on a sob and hung up.

He was at Patty's. He was hurt, and he was at Patty's. And she was nursing him and taking care of him and loving him....

Mandelyn burst into tears. Somehow, she was going to have to stop crying. Her heart was breaking.

She didn't eat breakfast or lunch. Around midafternoon she heard the sound of a car coming up the driveway.

She looked out the window and was shocked to see Patty's truck pulling up at the front door. Her eyes flashed. She wouldn't answer the doorbell. She wouldn't even talk to the other woman! Patty had Carson now, what else did she want?

Patty rang the bell and Mandelyn ignored her.

"Mandy!" Patty called. "Mandy, I know you're in there!'

"Go away!" Mandelyn called back, her voice wobbling. "I've got an awful headache. I can't talk to you!"

"Well, you're going to," Patty said stubbornly. "Shall I break a window?"

Mandelyn decided that another broken window would be too much trouble. Reluctantly, she opened the door.

Patty paused, shocked by the other woman's pale features.

"What do you want?" Mandelyn asked. Her voice sounded hoarse.

"I came to see about you," Patty said, surprised. "Angie said you had a migraine, and I thought you might want me to go to the pharmacy for you."

"You've already got one patient, just take care of him and leave me alone."

Patty moved closer, eyeing her friend closely. "Mandy, what's wrong?" she asked softly.

That was the straw that broke the camel's back. Mandelyn started crying again, and couldn't stop. Her body shook with broken sobs.

"Oh, Mandy, don't, I can't stand to see you like this," Patty pleaded, helping her to sit down in the living room. "What's wrong? Please, tell me!"

Mandelyn shook her head. "Nothing."

"Nothing." Patty looked toward the ceiling. "Carson takes his car into the swimming pool with him and you play hookey from work with a nonexistent headache, and nothing's wrong."

"You've got him now, what do you care what happens to me?" Mandelyn ground out, glaring at her.

"I've got him? Him, who? Carson?" Her eyes widened. "You think I'm after Carson?"

Mandelyn dabbed at her eyes. "Aren't you? He did it all for you, you know. Learning all about culture, and going to ballets and making fun of ballerinas and fixing up his house. You ought to be proud of yourself! He didn't think he was good enough for you the way he was, so he got me to give him lessons in etiquette!"

Patty's mouth opened. "Carson isn't in love with me!"

"Of course he is," Mandelyn said with trembling lips. "And I wish you every happiness!"

"Me? What about you?" Patty shot back. "You went away for the weekend with Jake!"

It was Mandelyn's turn to look shocked. "I went to Phoenix... alone."

Patty flushed. "Oh." She glared. "But you were all over him at my party."

"We were consoling each other," Mandelyn said wearily. "I suggested maybe he could learn to play a guitar and sing like Carson, and he said maybe I could go to veterinarian's school...."

"Jake was jealous?" Patty asked. "Of me?"

"Boy, are you dense," Mandelyn grumbled. "Of course he was jealous. Mad at Carson, mad at you. He asked me to dance so he wouldn't have to watch the two of you together. And when you kissed Carson, I thought he was going to go wild."

Patty's eyes misted. "Oh, my," she whispered.

A dawning realization made Mandelyn's tears dry up. "Patty... it's Jake, isn't it?"

"It's always been Jake," Patty confessed. She stared down at her jeans. "Since I was a teenager. But he wouldn't give me the time of day. I thought after I went away, maybe he'd miss me, but he didn't even write or call me. And when I came back here, I found all sorts of excuses to go out to the ranch, but he didn't notice. At the party I'd just about given up. I was hurting so much I couldn't stand it, and Carson knew and he played up to me to try to make Jake jealous. But I thought it backfired, because Jake wouldn't come near me. Last night, when I got Carson out of jail and took him home with me, Jake came to the front door and raised hell. I yelled back at him, and I thought it was all over. But now..."

"Jake loves you," Mandelyn whispered.

"Yes, I think he might," Patty faltered tearfully. "But why won't he admit it?"

"He's Carson's foreman. He isn't an educated man. And you've a degree. Maybe he doesn't feel worthy."

"I'll soon rid him of that silly notion, wait and see." Patty grinned. "I'll seduce him."

Mandelyn blushed wildly and Patty laughed.

"You might try that yourself," she suggested gently. "The way Carson lets you lead him around, I don't think he'd be able to stop you."

"I don't feel that way about Carson. I just feel guilty." The flush got worse. Mandelyn stared down at her shoes. "He hates me."

"Oh, sure he does."

"But he does!" Mandelyn wailed. She blurted out the whole painful story through a mist of tears. "I could just die! I hurt him and he could have been killed. I'd never have forgiven myself."

"Carson's tough," Patty said. "At least, he's tough with everyone but you."

"He's nice to you," Mandelyn reminded her.

"Oh, Carson and I go back a long way. We grew up together. I love him like a brother, and he knows it. But he's never been with anyone the way he is with you, honey. You must be the only person in Sweetwater who doesn't know that Carson's in love with you."

Mandelyn stared at her friend as if she'd lost her senses. Her eyes widened and her heart began to race.

"Didn't you ever wonder why he'd let you save people from him when he was drinking?" Patty asked, her eyes soft.

"Because I wasn't afraid of him," she replied.

Patty shook her head. "Because he would have done anything for you. We all knew it. And he'd sit and stare at you and have the damndest lost look on his face...."

"But... but he said there was a woman." Mandelyn hesitated. "He said she wouldn't have him the way he was, that he wanted to change and get cultured so that he could have a chance with her."

"He was talking about you," Patty said. "You, with your genteel background and your exquisite manners. It was like wishing for a star, and he must have known all along how impossible it was. But I guess he had to try."

Mandelyn felt as if someone had hit her over the head with a mallet. Carson loved her?

"Don't feel so bad," Patty said. "He'll get over it. He's almost back to normal this morning. Once he's realized what a silly idea it was, he'll come around, and you two will be friends again. Carson doesn't hold grudges. He'll thank you for having brought him to his senses." She stood up, grinning. "Imagine, you and Carson. That would be something, wouldn't it? The debutante and the outlaw. Wow!" She stretched. "Well, I'll never be able to tell you how grateful I am to know how Jake really feels. And don't you torment yourself about Carson. You only helped him see the light. He'll be okay. He's mostly just hung over."

"Would you...tell him I said I'm sorry?" she asked.

Patty studied her. "Wouldn't you like to come with me and tell him yourself?"

"No!" Mandelyn took a steadying breath. "No, I don't think so. It's too soon yet."

"Well, I'll relay the message. Feel better now? He isn't hurt. He's just dented."

Mandelyn nodded. "Thanks for coming by. I'm sorry I was ratty."

"No problem. I know what guilt can do to people. Say, you weren't getting sweet on Carson, were you?"

"Who me?" Mandelyn laughed nervously. "As you said, that would be something, wouldn't it?"

"A pretty wild match. What interesting kids you'd have. Okay, I'm going!" she laughed when Mandelyn started to look homicidal. "See you!"

Mandelyn sat by the window for a long time, thinking over what Patty had said. Bits and pieces of conversation came back to her, and she began to realize that it might have been true. Carson might have been falling in love with her. But whatever he'd felt before, he hated her now. He hated her for trying to live in the past with Ben, and for what she'd said to him at the ballet. He hated her for making him feel worthless and savage.

She fixed herself a light supper, trying to decide what to do. Her life was so empty now that she didn't know how she was going to survive. Perhaps she could go back to Charleston.

That thought appealed for only a few minutes. No, she couldn't leave Sweetwater. She couldn't leave Carson. Even if she only caught glimpses of him for the rest of her life, she couldn't bear being half a country away from him.

Several times, she went to the telephone and stared at it, wanting to call him, wanting to apologize. Or just to hear his voice. Finally, after dark, she dialed Patty's number.

"Hello," Patty said cheerfully.

"It's Mandelyn. Is...is Carson still there?"

"No, honey, he went home to nurse his bruises alone," Patty said. "He's feeling pretty low, though. You might try him there."

"Okay. Thanks."

"My pleasure," Patty murmured, and a male voice laughed softly in the background.

Mandelyn hung up, smiling faintly. It had sounded like Jake's voice, and she was glad that for Patty, at least, the long wait was over.

She dialed Carson's number and waited and waited until finally he picked it up.

"Hello," he said deeply, in a defeated kind of voice.

She was afraid he'd hang up on her. So she only said, very softly, "I'm sorry."

There was a long pause. "Why apologize for telling the truth?" he asked coldly.

At least he was talking to her. She sat down and leaned back against the sofa with her eyes closed. "How are you?"

"I'll live," he said curtly.

She couldn't think of anything to say. Except, maybe, "I love you." Because she did, so desperately. Patty had said that he loved her, but those days were gone for good. She knew she'd killed the delicate feelings he had for her.

"Do...do you need anything?" she asked hesitantly.

"Not from you, Mandelyn."

She knew that, but hearing it hurt. She swallowed down the tears. "I just wanted to see how you were. Good night."

She started to hang up, but he said her name in a way that made her toes curl up.

"Yes?" she whispered.

There was a long pause and she held her breath, hoping against hope for some crumb, some tiny clue that he still cared.

"Thanks for the lessons," he said after a minute. "I'll put them to good use."

"You're welcome," she replied, and hung up. Maybe Patty was wrong, she thought desperately. Maybe there was a woman neither of them knew about, a woman in Phoenix or some other town. And that thought tortured her long into the night.

Chapter Nine

The next few days were agonizing ones for Mandelyn. She lost her appetite for food, for living itself. For the first time, work wasn't enough to sustain her. And her memories of Ben, which had kept her going for years, had become nothing more than pleasant episodes from the past. She missed Carson. It was like having half of her body cut away and trying to live on what was left.

Once, she accidentally ran into him in the local fast-food restaurant. She'd stopped to get a cold drink as she walked back to her office after an appointment, and he was just coming out.

Her heart leapt up into her throat and she dropped her eyes. She couldn't even look at him. She turned around and went back the way she'd come without bothering about the cold drink. The look in his eyes had been chilling enough.

The second week, Patty stopped by the house to invite Mandelyn to go with her to the Sweetwater Rodeo.

"Come on," Patty coaxed. "You've been moping around for days. You need some diversion."

"Well..."

"You can go with Jake and me," she coaxed, grinning. "Things are going very well indeed in that department, by the way. I've almost got him hooked."

Mandelyn smiled. "I'm happy for you. I really am." But she couldn't bear the thought of driving in the pickup with Jake and hearing him talk about Carson. "I've got something to do earlier in town, though, so I'll just drive in and meet you there. Okay?"

"Okay."

She imagined Carson would be there, and she almost backed out at the last minute. But he'd be a competitor, as he usually was, and she wouldn't get close to him. She'd be able to see him, though. And the temptation was just too much for her hungry heart. Just to see him would be heaven.

She left her house fifteen minutes before the rodeo started and had a devil of a time finding a parking space at the fairgrounds. She managed to wedge her car in beside a big pickup and left it there, hoping she could get out before the owner of the pickup wanted to leave.

Patty waved to her from the front of the bleachers, where she was sitting beside Jake, his arm around her.

"Just in the nick of time," Patty said. "Better late than never, though."

"I couldn't find a parking spot. Hi, Jake," Mandelyn said as she sat down next to Patty. It was as if they had changed roles for the day—Patty was in a green print sundress and Mandelyn in jeans and boots and a blue tank top with her hair loose and sunglasses perched atop her head.

"Hi, Miss Bush," Jake said with a wicked smile. "I didn't know you liked rodeos."

"I like a lot of strange things these days," she returned. "Looks like you didn't need to learn the guitar after all."

Jake laughed and hugged Patty close. "Good thing, since I've got ten thumbs." He glanced toward her curiously. "Boss is riding today."

Her heartbeat faltered. "Is he?"

"In the steer wrestling and bronc riding. He's been practicing. We got two steers with permanently wrenched necks and one poor old bronc with a slipped disk."

"Nasty old Carson," Mandelyn said.

"I expect he'll take top money."

Mandelyn glanced around the ring, looking for a city woman somewhere. "Doesn't he have a cheering section with him?" she asked with barely concealed curiosity.

Jake and Patty exchanged amused glances. "Sure. Right here. We're it."

Mandelyn glared toward the dirt ring. "Amazing. I would have thought the object of his affections would be around somewhere. How's the house looking?"

"Just great," Jake returned. "He's kind of lost interest, though. Says it's no use anymore."

"There isn't any woman," Patty murmured under her breath. "I've told you already, it was you."

Mandelyn's face went hot and red. "Not now."

"Do you stop loving people just because you get angry with them?" Patty asked.

No, Mandelyn thought miserably. She'd never stop loving Carson. But what good would that do her? She'd just die of unrequited love, that was all.

The bronc riding competition was exciting. Most of the cowboys who participated drew good mounts, and the scores were high. But when Carson exploded into the arena on a horse named "TNT," groans were heard all around.

He rode magnificently, Mandelyn thought dreamily, watching his lean figure. His batwing chaps flew, his body whipped elegantly, gracefully, as it absorbed the shock of the bronc's wild motions. And by the time the horn blew, everybody knew that top money was going to Carson that day.

"Damn, isn't he good?" Jake laughed.

"I thought you'd be riding this time," Mandelyn remarked.

Jake looked down at Patty with a dreamy expression. "No. I've got more important things on my mind."

Patty blushed and snuggled closer and Mandelyn felt empty and cold and alone.

The sun beat down as rider after rider competed in bulldogging and calf roping. And then came steer wrestling. Carson was the last competitor, and there was a wild cheer as he came down off the horse squarely in front of the long horns of the animal. He dug in his heels, gave a quick, hard twist with his powerful arms, and the steer toppled onto the ground. Applause filled the bleachers, but Mandelyn was holding her breath as Carson got to his feet. The bull headed straight for him.

"No!" she screamed, leaping to her feet. "Carson!"

But it was all unnecessary. Lithe as a cat, he was onto the fence rail even as the animal charged. The rodeo clown made a great production of heading the steer off, finally leaping into a barrel and letting the animal work its frustration off by rolling him around.

Mandelyn managed to sit back down, but her face was white. Patty put an arm around her.

"Hey," she said gently. "He's been doing this a long time. He's okay."

"Yes, of course he is," Mandelyn said, swallowing down her fear. She clasped her hands tight in her lap and sat stiffly until the end of the competitions.

Later, she was about to head for her car when Patty caught her arm and tugged her along the aisle behind the pens. Carson was just loading his horse into the trailer behind the ranch pickup, and Jake went forward to shake his hand.

"Hey, boss, you done good." Jake grinned. "Congratulations."

"And you kept saying you were too old," Patty added, hugging him. "I was proud of you."

He hugged her back, smiling down at her in a way that twisted Mandelyn's heart. At least he and Patty were still friends. She hadn't wanted to come this close; she hadn't wanted to have to talk to him.

He looked up and saw her and his face froze. His expression went from sunshine to thunderstorm in seconds.

"We're going to see Billy for a minute," Patty called. "Be right back!"

She dragged Jake away, looking smug and triumphant. Mandelyn twisted a knot in the necklace she was wearing while Carson glared at her.

"You ... did very well," she said, hating the long silence.

Around them, animals snorted and whinnied, and there was a loud buzz of conversation among the milling cowboys.

"I didn't expect to find you at a rodeo," he said, lighting a cigarette. "It isn't exactly your thing, is it?"

"I like rodeos, actually," she returned. Her eyes went down to his opened shirt, and there was a red welt across his chest, visible through the mat of black curling hair. "Carson, you're hurt!" she burst out, moving close to him with wide, frightened eyes. "The bull got you...!" She reached out her fingers to touch it, and even as they made brief, electric contact with his skin, he'd caught her wrist bruisingly hard and pushed her away.

His eyes blazed like blue lightning. "Don't touch me, damn you!" he whispered furiously.

Her face went white. She could feel every single drop of blood draining out of it as she stared at him, horrified. So it was that bad. She was so repulsive to him that he couldn't even stand to have her hands on him now.

She wanted to crawl off and die. Tears burst from her eyes and a sob tore out of her throat.

She whirled and ran sightlessly through the crowd, crying so hard that she didn't hear Carson's wild exclamation or his furious footsteps behind her. She pushed people aside, jumped over saddles and trailer hitches and ran until her lungs felt like bursting. She wanted to go home. She wanted to get away. It was the only thought in her tortured mind.

She rounded the corner of the fence and squeezed by the pickup and into the front seat of her car. She was so blinded by tears that she could hardly see how to get the key into the ignition, but she managed it. She'd just started the car and was fumbling it into reverse when the door was jerked open and a lean, angry hand flashed past her to turn off the ignition and pull out the key.

"You little fool, you'll kill yourself trying to drive in that condition!" Carson said harshly. He was breathing hard as he stared down at her furiously.

The tears grew more profuse. "What the hell does it matter?" she asked brokenly. "I don't care if I die!"

"Oh, God," he ground out. He eased himself into the front seat beside her, facing her. His hands framed her face and he brought her mouth under his, tasting tears and mint and trembling lips. And the sob that rose from her throat went into his hard mouth, mingled with his rough breath.

He eased her head back against the seat with the pressure of his lips. His tongue caressed her, probed into the soft sweet darkness of her mouth. His sweaty chest pressed against her soft breasts and she could feel the hardness of muscle and the warmth of flesh and the wild thunder of his heart.

It was so sweet. So sweet, after all the long days and nights of wanting and needing and loving and pain. She slid her hands over his shoulders, up into the thick dampness of his hair and sighed shakily as her mouth opened and answered the tender pressure of his own.

His lips lifted, then came down again,

kissing away the tears and the pain while she sobbed softly and tried to stop crying.

"Carson," she whispered achingly.

"It's all right," he whispered back. His hands trembled on her face. He kissed her again, so tenderly that it hurt, and she moaned.

"I'm so hungry...for you," she moaned. "So hungry...for your mouth, your... hands."

"Baby..." he protested.

She crushed her mouth against his, drowning in sensual pleasure as he answered the hard kiss. His arms slid under her, pulling, crushing, and she thought if she died now, it would be all right. Life would never offer anything more beautiful than this, than Carson wanting her.

A long time later, she felt his mouth lift, and the breeze cooled her moistened lips. Her eyes opened, dark gray, still hungry, worshipping his face.

His nostrils flared. His own eyes were fierce and hot with unsatisfied passion.

"I want ... to have you," she whispered softly, searching his eyes.

His eyes closed. His teeth clenched. "It's no good! It won't change anything!"

"It will give you peace," she said, smoothing his hard face gently.

His eyes opened again, searching hers, and there was pain and hunger and loneliness in them.

She managed a tremulous smile. "Patty said once that I should seduce you. That you'd probably let me."

His fingers traced her mouth, unsteady and gentle. "That would be one for the books, wouldn't it? A shy little virgin seducing an outlaw like me?"

"Would you like it?" she whispered, wide-eyed.

He trembled before he could get his body under control, and she touched his hair, his face, with hands that loved the feel of him.

"I'd be...very careful with you," she said unsteadily, on a nervous laugh. "I wouldn't even let you get pregnant, I promise."

He burst out laughing, but his eyes were solemn and quiet. "Mandy..."

"Please," she whispered, beyond pride.

His eyes closed and he muttered a harsh word. "Look, it's no use," he said after a minute. "You and I are too different. Desire...it fades. So I want you. And you want me. But if we had each other, it wouldn't solve the problem. It would only make things unbearable." He sighed roughly and put her away from him. "No, honey. You go your own way. Someday you'll find some cultured dude with fancy manners and you'll live happily ever after. I was a fool to think anything would change. Goodbye, Mandelyn."

He got out of the car and left her sitting there, staring after him. She thought about what he'd said and a slow, easy smile came to her lips. That one tremor had given him away. She dried her tears and drove back to the house. She had things to do.

About midnight, she had a nice warm bath and doused herself in a faint, subtle perfume. She powdered her smooth, pink body and pulled on a button-up yellow dress, and nothing else. She brushed her hair until it shone. Then she slid into her sandals and got in her car and drove to Carson's house.

The lights were all off. She ran up onto the front porch, sure that the boys were all gone because it was Saturday night. She smiled wickedly as she thought about what she was going to do. Drastic situations called for drastic measures, and nobody had ever been this desperate, she decided. She knocked hard on the door, noticing that the wood-work was freshly painted. The porch looked nice. Very white and different, and there was a white porch swing and rocking chairs, too. She approved of the renovation.

There were muffled curses and thuds as she knocked again. The door flew open and Carson stood there, in the lighted room, without a stitch of clothing on his power-fully muscled, hair-roughened body.

Chapter Ten

Carson blinked, staring at her as if he thought he was having a dream. "Mandy?" he asked softly.

She was just adjusting to the sight of him. It had been a wild shock, although he was as perfect as a man could possibly be, and her eyes were only just able to drag themselves back up to his shocked face.

He stood aside, running a hand through his disheveled dark hair, just staring at her. She opened the screen door, her heart pounding, and walked into the living room. It was as much a shock as Carson. The sparse, worn furniture was gone, replaced by heavy oak pieces with brocade fabric in cream and chocolate. The brown carpet was thick; the curtains were of the same fabric as the upholstery on the chairs. And the beautiful fireplace had been renovated and was the showpiece she'd once thought it could be.

"The house is lovely," she remarked breathlessly, forcing her eyes to stay on his face.

"What are you doing here at this time of night?" he burst out.

Her eyes glanced down and up again and she flushed. "Getting anatomy lessons."

He glanced down, too, and smiled ruefully. "Well, you should have called first."

"I guess so."

"Want me to put my pants on, or is the shock wearing off?"

She searched his blue eyes, hesitating. It had seemed so easy when she was thinking about it. And now it was becoming more impossible by the minute. The longer she waited, the weaker her nerve became. He needed a shave, but he looked vital and exquisitely masculine and she wanted to touch him all over that bronzed skin.

She moved closer to him, watching the way his eyes narrowed warily.

"I...want you...to come to bed with me," she faltered.

He glared at her. "I told you this afternoon how I felt about that," he said curtly.

"Yes, I know." She reached out and touched his chest, watching the way he stiffened. His hands caught her, but she trailed her fingers slowly down his body and his hold weakened. His body trembled and jerked.

"Don't," he whispered huskily.

It was so easy. Easier than she'd dreamed. Heady with success, she pressed her body against his and reached up to coax his head down.

"Help me," she whispered. She eased her mouth onto his and kissed him tenderly. She loved his immediate response to her. He tasted of whiskey. It was a little disturbing at first, but the warm hardness of his mouth got through to her and she became accustomed to the strong taste.

His hands caught her shoulders. "Mandy, we can't," he breathed roughly. "You're a virgin, for God's sake!"

"Yes, you'll be my first man," she whispered. "The very first."

That made his hands tremble and she stood on tiptoe, brushing her body softly against his so that something predictable and awesome happened to him. She sighed and moaned.

"It's going to be so beautiful," she said at his lips. "The most beautiful night..."

She left him long enough to close and lock the door. Then she went back to him, where he stood frozen and waiting, and reached up her arms.

"Would you carry me?" she whispered.

He bent like a man in a trance and lifted her tenderly in his hard arms. She nestled her face into his throat, feeling the thunderous beat of his pulse there, feeling his taut body absorb the shock of his footsteps as he carried her into the darkened bedroom and laid her down on his rumpled bed.

"Honey..." he began in a strangled voice.

"Here," she said, drawing his hands to the buttons of her dress.

He muttered something, and his fingers trembled as he fumbled them open. She sat up, sliding the dress off her body. She lay back, her body pale in the patch of moonlight coming through the window. She held out her arms.

"Come here, darling," she whispered. She wasn't even afraid. She wanted him. She wanted a child with him. And tonight she was going to make sure she had that, if nothing else. If he sent her away, she wanted at least the hope, the tiny hope, of having a part of him.

"Mandy," he groaned. He lay down on the bed with her like a lamb going to slaughter.

"It's all right," she whispered. She trembled a little when his hands moved down her thighs and back up over her flat stomach and her soft breasts.

"You're afraid," he whispered.

"It's very mysterious right now," she explained quietly. "I... I know the mechanics, but I don't know how it's going to feel, you see. Will... Carson, will it hurt me very much?" she whispered.

"We don't have to do it," he said.

"I have to," she breathed. "I have to!"

"Why?" he asked.

His hands were fascinated with her body, and she stretched like a cat being stroked, loving their rough tenderness. "I want a baby," she whispered. "I want your baby."

He shuddered wildly. His breath caught and he buried his face against her body, groaning helplessly.

Yes, she thought, drawing him closer, yes, that had done it. Now he wouldn't be able to stop, or stop her. It would happen now, because she'd stirred him in an unbearable way.

His mouth found hers hungrily, and his hands began to touch her in new, shocking ways. She trembled and twisted and moaned, and still his hands tormented her.

His mouth went on a trembling journey of exploration that left not one inch of her untouched, that made her cry out and whisper things to him that would have shocked her speechless in daylight.

When she felt his weight on her, she stiffened a little, and his hands brushed back her damp hair, calming her.

"I won't take you in a rush," he promised tenderly. "Mandy, close your eyes for a minute. I'm going to turn on the light."

"No...!"

"Yes," he whispered, brushing his mouth over her eyes as he reached out to turn on the light at the head of the bed.

Her eyes opened, shocked, frightened and although she knew he was too committed to draw away, she was afraid the starkness of the light might make him stop.

His hands smoothed her hair, touched her hot cheeks. His eyes adored her, glazed with desire, bright with passion and hunger.

"I asked you this once before. Let me watch," he whispered shakily. "You came in here a virgin, and we're about to do some-

thing extraordinary together. Let me ...
watch it happen to you ... please.''

Her body trembled, but she didn't say a
word. Her hands touched his broad, perspiring shoulders, his chest, his face. She felt
him move and her eyes dilated. She stiffened, but his fingers touched her hair again,
soothing, comforting as his hips eased down.

"No," he whispered when she tried to
move away. His voice shook, but his smile
was steady, his eyes were ... loving her.

"Oh," she whispered sharply, staring
straight into his eyes as his body locked with
hers.

"Yes," he said, shuddering, his face
clenching. "Oh, God, yes, yes ... yes!"

Something incredible was happening. She
couldn't believe the intimacy of it. Her nails
were biting into him and she didn't even realize it. Her body forgot that it had a brain
and began to entice him, incite him. It
arched and forced a deeper intimacy that
began as pain and suddenly became easy and
sweet and achingly tender.

"Now," she whispered mindlessly. "Now, I...belong...to you...!"

"Baby...was there a time...when you didn't?" he bit off. His mouth burned into hers, hot and wet and hungry, and his body began to find a new rhythm with hers. She felt his hands, holding her hips, showing her how. She closed her eyes and let her body teach her what to do, her hands touching, her mouth whispering into his. Storms. Sunlight. Wild breeze and sweet peace. Open fields and running feet. A surge. A scream. Hers. And all too soon she felt conscious again. Carson lay shuddering helplessly on her trembling body, his voice shaking as if he were in unholy torment, whispering her name like a litany.

She reached up to cradle him, to comfort him. Her eyes opened and there was the ceiling, the light fixture. She moved and felt his body move, and realized that they were still part of each other. She caught her breath at the beauty of it.

It took him a long time to calm down. She

stroked him and soothed him, and wondered at the force of his passion.

"It had been a long time, hadn't it?" she whispered softly.

He levered himself over her and searched her misty eyes with regret and pain in his own. "I took you," he said jerkily.

"Not exactly," she murmured with a warm smile.

"For God's sake...!"

She arched up and kissed his mouth softly, tenderly, smiling against it.

"Don't..."

Her hips twisted sensuously under his and something that should have been impossible, suddenly wasn't. Deliciously surprised, she closed her eyes and kissed him harder.

"Oh, God," he ground out. And then he stopped talking. She locked her arms behind his neck and held the kiss until the world exploded around them again. Finally, exhausted, they slept in each other's arms.

She awoke before he did, slipping back into her dress while she studied his long, elegant body on the bed. He was beautiful, she decided. Not cultured and citified and well-mannered. But beautiful and sensitive and he'd make the most marvelous father....

Her face burned as she recalled the long night. Well, it was too late for regrets now. He'd marry her. He'd have to. Because if he didn't, she fully intended to move in with him anyway.

She went into the clean, neat new kitchen and found an equally new refrigerator that had been recently filled. She cooked eggs and bacon and thick, fluffy biscuits and made a pot of coffee. When she'd set the table, she went back into the bedroom.

He was sprawled on his back, still sound asleep. She sat down beside him and bent to brush her mouth slowly over his.

"Baby..." he whispered hungrily, and reached up to kiss her lips. Then he stiffened. His eyes opened. He looked up at Mandelyn and his face went white. "Oh, my God. It happened."

"You might sound a little less horrified," she murmured drily. "You seemed to enjoy it enough last night."

His hands went to his eyes and he rubbed them. "I had a bottle of whiskey and then I went to bed. And…" His eyes opened. "You seduced me!"

She sighed. "That's what they all say," she said with mock weariness.

He sat up in bed and stared straight into her eyes. "You seduced me!" he repeated roughly.

"Well, you needn't make such heavy weather of it, Carson, I'm surely not the first woman who ever did," she reminded him reasonably.

"You were a virgin!"

She grinned. "Not anymore."

"Oh, God!"

She got up with a sigh. "I can see that you're just not in the mood to discuss this right now. So why don't you come and have breakfast?"

He threw his legs over the side of the bed and stared at her departing figure. "Why?"

She turned at the doorway, her eyes soft and possessive. "Don't you know?" And she walked out.

He made his way into the room minutes later. He was dressed now, in jeans and a brown patterned shirt and boots. But he looked half out of humor and bitterly regretful. He glared at her as he sat down.

"What a horrible expression," she remarked, handing him the platter of scrambled eggs.

"Aren't you even upset?" he burst out.

"Should I be? I mean, you did drag me into bed with you and . . ."

"I did not!" he growled. "You did it, you crazy little fool!"

"That's no way to talk to the mother of your children," she said calmly and poured coffee into the thick mug beside his plate.

"Children . . ." He put his face into his hands. "You knocked me so off balance I couldn't even hold back. What if I got you pregnant?"

"I like children." She smiled softly. "Just think, Carson, if we have a little girl, I can teach her how to be a lady. And if he's a boy, you can teach him the guitar."

He looked up with bloodshot eyes, staring as if he didn't believe what he was hearing. "Mandy?"

Her fingers reached out and brushed over the back of his with an adoring pressure. She searched his eyes and all the amusement went out of hers. "I love you," she whispered. "I love you more than anything else in the world, Carson. And if you'll just let me live with you, I won't even ask you for anything. I'll cook and clean and have babies and you won't know I'm around, I'll be so quiet . . . !"

"Come here," he said in a voice that shook with emotion. "Oh, God, come here!"

She went around the table, to be dragged down into his arms and kissed to within an inch of her life.

"Love . . . you," he groaned against her mouth. "So much, for so . . . long. I was dying. . . ."

"Darling, darling!" she whispered, clinging, loving, worshipping him with her hands, her mouth.

He couldn't seem to get enough of her soft, eager mouth. He tasted it and touched it and kissed it until it was tender from the rough pressure. His mouth slid down her body, against her breasts.

"It was me," she guessed, closing her eyes as she remembered the pain she'd caused him. "It was me you were being tutored for, because ... because you thought I wouldn't want you."

His arms tightened. "Eight years, Mandelyn," he said unsteadily. "Eight years, I worshipped you. And it got to where I couldn't eat or sleep or live for loving you. I wanted to fit into your world, so that I'd have a chance with you."

"And as it turns out, yours suits me very well," she said humbly. "You were right, Carson. Your world is real and honest and the people don't put on airs. I like it better than mine." She clung to him. "Let me live with you."

"Always," he promised. "All my life. All yours. But first," he said curtly, lifting his head, "we get married. Pronto."

Her eyebrows arched. "Why the rush?"

"As if you didn't know, you little witch," he said. His big hand pressed against her stomach and he kissed her roughly. "Whispering that to me last night, when I was doing my damnest to keep my head, to stop myself. Whispering that you wanted my baby. And I went crazy in your arms. You were damned lucky I didn't hurt you."

"I wouldn't have cared," she murmured contentedly. "It was so sweet, so heavenly. Oh, Carson, I loved you and I knew, I thought, I hoped you loved me. And you were so tender, and I wanted to make it perfect for you."

"It was perfect all right. Both times," he added drily. "After we've been married a few years, remind me to tell you that what happened was impossible, will you?"

She grinned. "You said yourself you'd been a long time without a woman."

"That wasn't why," he said. His eyes held hers. "It was wanting you. Obsessively."

She kissed his closed eyelids. "I felt the same way. I could have died the night we went to the ballet. Those things I said...and when I heard about your driving the car into the pool, I got sick all over. I wanted to go down on my knees and apologize. I missed you and I loved you and I knew I'd die without you.''

"I felt the same way," he confessed. He drew her close and held her securely on his lap. "Then yesterday, at the rodeo, you touched me and I wanted you so badly that..." He sighed. "I got the shock of my life when you started crying after I pushed you away. I was terrified that you were going to get in the car and have a wreck. I trampled two people getting to you. And then I knew just how bad I had it—that I was going to waste away without you. I knew you wanted me, then. But I didn't think you loved me." His eyes searched hers. "I thought you came to me last night out of pity."

She shook her head. "It was love."

"I should have realized that you'd never give yourself without it." He sighed.

"You're much too fastidious for love affairs. Even with wild men you desire."

"You're not wild," she murmured. "You're just a maverick. I love you the way you are, Carson. I wouldn't change one single thing about you. Of course, I'll never go with you to another ballet . . . oh!"

He pinched her and laughed uproariously. "Yes, you will," he murmured. "We'll take the kids. I want them to be polished. Not like their father."

"They'll have a lovely father," she sighed, kissing him again. "When are we going to get married?"

"Today."

She sat up, and he pulled her back down. "We'll drive down to Mexico," he said gently. His eyes searched hers. "It has to be done right. Making love to you without my ring on your finger doesn't sit well. Does it?"

She lowered her eyes to his broad chest. "No," she confessed.

He tilted up her chin. "But I don't have one single regret about last night. That was the consummation. That was the wedding vows. Now we make it right.''

Her fingers touched his mouth. ''I adore you,'' she whispered passionately. Her gray eyes searched his blue ones. ''I want you so much.''

His hand touched her stomach, flattened, caressed it. ''Tonight,'' he whispered. ''After we're married. It will be better this time. Slower. Sweeter.''

She trembled and leaned toward him, but he shook his head with a tender smile. ''First you marry me. Then you sleep with me,'' he said.

''We got it backwards.''

''We'll get it right this time,'' he promised, smiling. ''Up you go. I want to call Patty and see if she and Jake will stand up with us.''

''They way things are going with them, it might be a double wedding,'' she laughed.

He looked down at her. ''I was jealous of Jake.''

"I was jealous of Patty. When she kissed you that night, I wanted to mop the floor with her."

He searched her eyes and smiled wickedly. "Yes. I saw that. It was the only glimmer of hope I had."

Her mouth fell open. She started to speak, but he bent and put his lips on hers. And since it felt so good, she gave up protesting and wound her arms around his neck. He might not be the world's most polished man, but he was the only one she would ever love.

They drove down to Mexico, and Mandelyn and Carson said their vows in muted, solemn voices while Jake and Patty looked on.

Mandelyn looked into his eyes while she spoke the words, and he couldn't seem to look away, even when it was time to slide the ring on her finger. He did it blindly, with amazing accuracy. And then he bent to kiss his wife.

It was a beautiful day, and Mandelyn felt like a fairy princess. She clung to Carson's lean hand, hardly believing all that had happened. When he suggested that the four of them stop by a bar on the other side of the border for a drink, she was too happy to protest.

"Isn't this nice?" Patty sighed as Carson and Jake went to get drinks. "I loved your wedding. Jake must have enjoyed it, too," she added with a grin, "because he proposed under his breath while you two were sealing the ceremony with that absurdly long kiss."

Mandelyn blushed. "I hope you'll be as happy as we are," she laughed.

"I hope so, too. Didn't it all work out..."

"What the hell do you mean, 'move over, Pop'?" Carson's deep, angry voice came across the room like a cutting whip and Mandelyn opened her mouth to say, "Oh, Carson, don't," when the sound of a hard fist hitting an even harder jaw echoed in the sudden silence.

Mandelyn gritted her teeth. "No," she groaned, watching Carson going at it with a man just his size. "Not on my wedding day. Not just before my wedding night!"

"Carson's tough," Patty promised her. "Quit worrying. It will be all right."

Just as she said that, a man who'd been standing beside Carson's opponent picked up a chair. Mandelyn's mouth flew open. Her temper flared like wildfire. That was her husband that ruffian was about to hit!

"Mandy, no!" Patty called.

But Mandelyn was already bounding over chairs. She picked up a vase from one of the tables and threw water, flowers and all into the face of the man holding the chair.

He sputtered, wiped himself off and glared at her. "Women's libber, huh?" he said curtly. "Okay, honey, put up your dukes."

"Whatever happened to chivalry?" Mandelyn wondered out loud. She brought her high heel down on the man's instep and when he bent over, she brought up her knee. The blow was apparently very painful, because he went sideways onto the floor.

She grinned, heady with success. "Hey, Carson . . ." she began.

Just about that time, the man who'd been trading blows with Carson took one too many hard rights and careened backwards into Mandelyn. He rammed against her and she fell headfirst into a huge planter full of ferns.

Wet, covered with dirt, she heard the sounds of the brawl escalating all around her as she struggled to get up again. As she raised her head, Carson came flying backwards from an uppercut and landed against her, and in she went again.

Somewhere there was a siren. And minutes later, she was extricated from the planter by a heavyset, blue-uniformed man who looked as if he had absolutely no sense of humor at all.

"We can explain all this," Mandelyn assured him in her most cultured voice.

"I'm sure you can, lady, but I assure you, I've heard it all before. Come along."

"But we just got married," she wailed, watching Carson being led out between two burly deputies.

"Congratulations," the uniformed man said blandly. "I'll show you both to the honeymoon suite."

As they waited to be booked Mandelyn leaned against the wall staring daggers at her new husband. Her hair was thick with dirt and traces of green leaves; her dress was ruined.

Carson cleared his throat and sighed. "Well, honey," he said with a grin, "you have to admit, I've given you a wedding day you'll never forget."

She didn't say anything but her eyes spoke volumes.

He moved closer, oblivious to the noise and confusion around them. "Mad at me?" he murmured.

"Furious, thanks," she replied.

"My Charleston lady," he whispered, smiling with such love that her poise fell apart.

"You horrible, horrible man," she murmured, "I love you so much!"

He laughed delightedly. "My poised little lady, right at home in a barroom brawl. My

God, you laid that cowboy flat! I've never been so proud of you...." He lifted his head and looked stern. "But never again, honey. I don't want you fighting, even to save me. Especially not now," he added. His gaze went to her waist. "We don't know yet, remember," he whispered tenderly.

She flushed and looked up into his eyes. She knew exactly what he meant.

He bent and kissed her very gently. She managed a watery smile.

"Oh, I hope I am," she breathed fervently.

His chest rose and fell heavily. "We can make sure, if you want," he replied in a voice hoarse with passion.

"Is it too soon?" she asked.

He shook his head. "Not at our ages. We'll just be spreading love around, that's all." He grinned.

She laughed. "You can sing lullabies," she said. "And I'll sit and listen."

"Remember that song I wrote— Choices?" he asked, searching her eyes. She nodded. "I wrote it for us. That's right," he added when she looked stunned. "I thought someday, if you ever started noticing me, I could sing it to you, and it might tell you something."

She sighed miserably. "And I was too busy being jealous of Patty to listen to the words," she mumbled.

"I'll sing it to you tonight, while we make love," he whispered.

"And here we are in jail," she moaned.

"Patty and Jake will be here any minute to bail us out," he promised. He grinned. "Don't you worry, honey. Everything's going to be fine. Next time, I won't hit, I'll just cuss. Okay?"

She burst out laughing, loving him with all her heart. "Okay. But don't change, will you?" she added seriously, searching his pale, glittering blue eyes. "Darling, I love you just the way you are."

He looked at her for a long time before he spoke. "I'm no gentleman."

"I'm no lady. Remember last night?" she whispered.

He trembled and kissed her quickly again.

Nearby, two slightly intoxicated men were staring at them. Mandelyn thought she recognized them from the brawl.

"Ain't that the blonde who threw the vase at me?" one asked the other, who squinted toward her.

"Yep. Looks like her."

"And kicked me on the foot and knocked me out with her knee?"

"The very same one."

The burly man grinned. "Lucky son of a gun," he slurred.

Carson glanced at him with a slow grin. "You don't know the half of it, pal," he murmured and bent his head again.

Mandelyn smiled, feeling as if she had champagne flowing through her body. "Darling, about that brawl . . ."

"What about it?" he murmured absently.

She grinned. "Could we do it again sometime?"

And that was the last thing she got to say until Jake and Patty came along to bail them out. Not that she minded. She was already making plans for the night and whispering them to a glowing new husband.

Take 3 of "The Best of the Best™" Novels FREE
Plus get a FREE surprise gift!

Special Limited-time Offer

Mail to The Best of the Best™

P. O. Box 609
Fort Erie, Ontario
L2A 5X3

YES! Please send me 3 free novels and my free surprise gift. Then send me 3 of "The Best of the Best™" novels each month. I'll receive the best books by the world's hottest romance authors. Bill me at the low price of $3.99 each—plus 25¢ delivery and GST*. That's the complete price and a savings of over 10% off the cover prices—quite a bargain! I understand that accepting the books and gift places me under no obligation ever to buy any books. I can always return a shipment and cancel at any time. Even if I never buy another book from Harlequin, the 3 free books and the surprise gift are mine to keep forever.

383 BPA AQY6

Name	(PLEASE PRINT)	
Address	Apt. No.	
City	Province	Postal Code

This offer is limited to one order per household and not valid to current subscribers.
*Terms and prices are subject to change without notice. All orders subject to approval.
Canadian residents will be charged applicable provincial taxes and GST.

CBOB-295   ©1990 Harlequin Enterprises Limited

New York Times Bestselling Author

LINDA LAEL MILLER

Imagine yourself in the wilds of Australia.
Imagine you are

JUST KATE

Kate Blake had never forgotten Sean Harris. But the brash,
brawny Australian was strictly off-limits. He was, after all,
the man who'd married her sister and the man her family
still blamed for her sister's death. He was the very last man
Kate had any business loving—and yet she couldn't quite
shake her attraction for him. Needing a change of pace, she
decided to take Sean up on his offer and visit the outback
and the nephew she'd never seen. But what she didn't count
on was *his* attraction for her.

Look for JUST KATE this September at your favorite retail outlet.

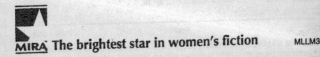

BARBARA BRETTON

Destiny's Child

Dakota Wylie was a typical twentieth-century woman living a typical twentieth-century life—chaotic! But it was calmer than the existence she found herself leading in eighteenth-century New Jersey with Patrick Devane. He was stubborn and cynical and thought her brazen and unladylike. But there was no denying the passion between them. Caught in a time of tumultuous change, Dakota and Patrick found their hearts on fire with hate as well as love. Now Patrick was accused of spying. And Dakota had to decide whether she had traveled two hundred years through time to lie with a man who was now branded an enemy....

Don't miss *Destiny's Child* this September, at your favorite retail outlet.

If you love the sensuous tales of

DIANA PALMER

Order now and receive more romantic stories
by one of MIRA's bestselling authors:

#48267	HEATHER'S SONG	$4.50	☐
#48268	FIRE AND ICE	$4.50	☐
#48269	THE AUSTRALIAN	$4.50	☐
#48292	SOLDIER OF FORTUNE	$4.50	☐
#48298	THE TENDER STRANGER	$4.50	☐
#48305	ENAMORED	$4.50 U.S	☐
		$4.99 CAN.	☐
#66009	THE RAWHIDE MAN	$4.99 U.S	☐
		$5.50 CAN.	☐
#66031	LADY LOVE	$4.99 U.S	☐
		$5.50 CAN.	☐

(limited quantities available on certain titles)

TOTAL AMOUNT	$
POSTAGE & HANDLING	$
($1.00 for one book, 50¢ for each additional)	
APPLICABLE TAXES*	$
TOTAL PAYABLE	$
(check or money order—please do not send cash)	

To order, complete this form and send it, along with a check or money order
for the total above, payable to MIRA Books, to: **In the U.S.:** 3010 Walden
Avenue, P.O. Box 9077, Buffalo, NY 14269-9077; **In Canada:** P.O. Box 636,
Fort Erie, Ontario, L2A 5X3.

Name: _____

Address: _____City: _____

State/Prov.: _____ Zip/Postal Code: _____

*New York residents remit applicable sales taxes.
Canadian residents remit applicable GST and provincial taxes.   MDPBL3

MIRA